TWO FOR ROMANCE

Lord Harcourt lifted an eyebrow. "I am intrigued, madam. What is it you wished to speak to me about?"

"The roses, my lord," Regina said. "They did, indeed, smell sweet."

"They met with your approval, then?"

"I should be hard to please if they had not. I believe I may safely say they are the most beautiful flowers I have ever received."

He leaned rather close to her and since Regina stood almost flush with the wall and had no place to retreat, she was obliged to endure his proximity with what calmness she could summon. When he spoke, his voice was hushed, almost a whisper. "There are those who feel the rose is too secretive a flower."

Regina felt pickles of sensation run up the back of her neck. "Secretive?"

"According to the florist, the rose hides its true beauty behind a protective covering."

"It . . . it does?"

"Without a doubt," he replied. "And the fellow informed me if I wished to see the *real* flower, I must carefully remove the outer petals that shield it."

Regina felt those prickles again.

Slowly, deliberately, Lord Harcourt touched the tip of his forefinger to one of the folds of her veil, then he traced the silken crease from somewhere near her temple to just above her madly beating heart. "Perhaps, he said, quietly, "it is you who should remove that protective covering . . ."

WATCH FOR THESE ZEBRA REGENCIES

THREE FOR BRIGHTON

Martha Kirkland

Zebra Books
Kensington Publishing Corp.

http://www.zebrabooks.com

ZEBRA BOOKS are published by

Kensington Publishing Corp.
850 Third Avenue
New York, NY 10022

Zebra and the Z logo Reg. U.S. Pat. & TM Off.

First Printing: February, 1998
10 9 8 7 6 5 4 3 2 1

Printed in the United States of America

In memory of our sweet Buffy
March 31, 1981–January 21, 1997

Chapter One

"No money! But that is absurd. Of course there is money. Ten thousand pounds does not just disappear."

Miss Regina Farrington searched the faces of her two young cousins, both of whom were dressed in mourning gowns of dove gray, edged around the neck and sleeves in black crepe. She hoped there was some mistake about their inheritance, but as she watched tears slip past the thick sooty lashes of Constance's sapphire blue eyes, Regina's hope began to fade.

"May I see the letter?" She asked the question of Miss Felicity Mitchell, a diminutive young lady of seventeen summers, for though she was the younger of the two sisters, hers was the stronger personality. "Perhaps you have misunderstood the lawyer's words."

"I only wish I had."

Moving away from the bow window where she had been polishing a handsome brass-banded telescope that stood upon a tripod, Felicity strode rather impatiently across the sitting room to fetch the letter from atop the black marble mantle piece.

"Read it for yourself," she said, handing over the single page bearing the ham-fisted scrawl of their deceased father's attorney. "See what you make of this lunacy."

Reading through the missive carefully, Regina concentrated on each word. When she had perused the final line, she made a strangled sound deep inside her throat and let the paper fall to the faded carpet. "It is true," she muttered between angry gasps. "The money is gone."

"Every last farthing," Felicity said.

Unable to keep her emotions in check a moment longer, Felicity began to pace the room, stopping only when she was beside a mahogany table that held several pieces of porcelain. Grabbing up one of the objects—a pretty blue Sevres bowl depicting a shepherdess with a beribboned staff in her hand—she turned and threw it with all her might, sending it crashing against the empty fireplace. Upon impact, the bowl seemed to explode, falling to the hearth in a hundred forlorn fragments.

At the sound, Constance jumped, then she began to cry in earnest. Hearing the sobs, Felicity, whose anger was now spent, ran to the little yellow settee and put her arms around her trembling sister.

"Forgive me," she said, "but it was either the shepherdess or me. And though I can boast of neither your height nor your beautiful figure, Constance, if I had exploded, I assure you I would have made a much bigger mess than the bowl."

Under normal circumstances, Constance would have laughed at her sister's foolishness, then uttered her usual platitude about important things coming in small packages, but it was a sign of her distress that she remained silent. Extricating herself from Felicity's embrace, she pushed back a strand of pale blond hair that had fallen free of the knot she wore atop her head. Staring beseechingly at Regina, she said, "What are we to do?"

Do? How could Regina answer such a question? She had been away from Byrn Park for five years, and though she had been reared under her uncle's roof, she had left as soon as she reached her majority, for she had always detested Sir Hubert Mitchell, the man who had ruined her mother's happiness.

Not content with separating his sister, who was also his ward, from the young lieutenant she loved, Sir Hubert had spent the next twenty years making Regina's mother rue the day she refused to marry to fill *his* coffer. Keeping her dependent upon him for the very food she and her daughter ate, he never missed an opportunity to vilify her before her child and others, constantly referring to her as a worthless drain upon his finances.

Not wishing to linger on these disturbing memories, Regina concentrated upon the question put to her by her cousin. "You must give me a moment to think about what is best to do, Constance, for I am still trying to understand how a man could risk an entire fortune on the exchange."

"More to the point," Felicity added, "how could a father swindle his own daughters of their dowries? Their very livelihoods?"

"Not *swindle*," Constance corrected. "That is such a harsh word. Surely Father only meant to—"

"He meant to do exactly as he pleased! When did he

not? He was an autocrat to his last breath, brooking no interference or gainsaying of his wishes.''

"Felicity," her sister cautioned softly, "one must not speak ill of the departed."

"I should like to know why not! Father's having succumbed to the influenza did not make him a saint. Can you tell me of even one instance where he showed the least concern for the needs or wants of those parties who would be most intimately affected by his actions?''

When Constance remained silent, Felicity answered for her. "No, you cannot, for he never did so. One has only to remember poor Aunt Anne. Surely you have not forgotten how Father ruined his own sister's life, forcing her to bend to his will. Or how he made it impossible for Regina to remain with us after our aunt's passing."

"I have not forgotten," Constance said.

"Now he has done his best to ruin our lives. Somehow Father found a way to set aside our maternal grandfather's will, gaining access to the ten thousand pounds that was to be divided between the two of us for our marriage portions. Without giving a thought to our welfare, he gambled our futures upon the exchange. Gambled and lost.'' Felicity stood and began to pace the room once again. "Not that such behavior should come as a surprise to those of us who have lived beneath his roof."

Regina, hearing the renewed anger in her cousin's voice, and noting the direction of her pacing, rose from her chair and hurried across the room, putting herself between the mahogany table and the angry girl. "I beg you, Felicity, spare the remaining porcelain."

Since Felicity was only slightly more than five feet tall, and weighed just under seven stone, even this mild show of force was sufficient to disuade her.

"You dare not smash another piece of the Sevres, for if the letter is correct, the house and everything in it now belong to your second cousin, Mr. George Mitchell. And should the new baronet choose to do so, he could turn you both out with only the clothes on your backs."

"Ha! As though we need concern ourselves with our cousin. The instant his wife sees Constance's beautiful face, you may mark my words, Gina, we shall be evicted from Byrn Park faster than the cat can lick her ear."

Regina was much struck by this view of the situation. "I had not even thought of that possibility."

She turned to look at her cousin. Constance Mitchell had been a lovely baby and an uncommonly pretty child, but now, at twenty, the young lady was an Incomparable. She was almost as tall as Regina and possessed a figure that was perfection itself. With pale blond hair that shimmered like purest silk, sapphire blue eyes fringed by long, sooty eyelashes, and skin like flawless alabaster, there was but one word for Constance—*breathtaking.*

No one seeing her could doubt that the gentlemen found her comely, or that their wives and sweethearts would perceive her as a threat. "If the new Lady Mitchell should take you in dislike, where will you go?"

Felicity answered for them both. "We do not know. We have talked of nothing else for days; unfortunately, I have been unable to devise a plan.

"What of you, Gina?" Constance asked. "After this condolence visit to us, do you return to Mrs. Phelps?"

Regina shook her head. When she had left Byrn Park five years ago, it was to become a paid companion to an elderly lady who resided in Maidstone. Now, however, that dear lady had found a new home in the quiet, beech-shaded church yard at St. Anne's.

Fortunately for Regina, Mrs. Phelps had performed one final act of kindness toward her companion; she had bequeathed her five hundred pounds. With that money to sustain her, Regina was not obliged to seek new employment immediately. Also, as a result of that bequest, she would now be able to realize her life's dream—her dream and that of her dear mother. She could search personally for her father.

Brighton! At the thought of her ultimate destination, Regina felt her heart quicken its pace in anticipation. She had been writing letters for years, searching for any information regarding her father, and now she had a very promising clue as to his whereabouts. A former military man named Farrington—a man whose age and background agreed with the details her mother had given her years ago—resided just outside the seaside town of Brighton.

To stem her rising excitement, Regina turned from the table of porcelains and walked over to look out the window that gave onto an expanse of the extensive park. She had forgotten the beauty of the Sussex Downs, where low rolling green hills seemed to extend into infinity and flocks of cloud-white sheep grazed placidly, adding to the feeling of serenity. "Odd," she muttered, "but it is so much prettier than I remembered."

"I beg your pardon?" Felicity asked.

"Forgive me, I was merely thinking aloud." Recalled to her surroundings, Regina returned her attention to her young cousin, studying her now as she had done Constance earlier.

The five years of Regina's absence had changed more than her perception of the countryside, it had changed her youngest cousin out of all recognition. Where she had left a schoolroom chit of twelve who was often mistaken for a lass of nine or ten, the person who stood before her now was a young lady full grown. Her cousin's light brown hair and gray eyes were legacies from Sir Hubert, but there the resemblance ended, for Felicity possessed an English rose complexion, a charming pixie's face, and a smile that lit up the room.

"And since I am already guilty of thinking aloud, Felicity, allow me to remark upon my surprise at seeing you. I cannot believe how grown up you are."

Assuming an air worthy of a duchess, the young lady stood straight, her head held high. "I am a full two inches taller than when you saw me last." Her boast completed, the irrepressible miss giggled then glanced down meaningfully at her reed-thin figure. "Unfortunately," she said, fluffing up the lawn fichu that crisscrossed her chest, "my growth *outward* is not what I had hoped it would be."

Regina could not stop herself from chuckling, for her cousin was as delightfully outspoken as ever. And as disarmingly truthful. Giving in to an impulse, she hurried across the room to embrace the minx. "I have missed you so," she said, her voice suddenly thick with emotion. "Both of you."

"And we have missed you, as well, but I noticed that you did not answer Constance's question. Is there some reason why you might not return to Mrs. Phelps?"

"You were always quick," Regina said. "I am not returning to Maidstone because Mrs. Phelps passed away five weeks ago."

Two pairs of eyes questioned her, but it was Constance who spoke. "So long ago, and you are but now returning to us?"

"At the request of Mrs. Phelps's nephew, I remained at the estate until such time as he and his wife could arrange their affairs in town and take up residence in Kent. I was packed and ready to leave when your letter arrived informing me of Uncle Hubert's demise.''

"Then your fate is much like ours," Constance said, tears threatening again. "You, too, have no place to go."

"Her fate is not at all like ours," Felicity corrected, "for she has experience as a companion, and will probably have glowing references from the Phelps family. We, on the other hand, are totally unemployable. I am too young and you are far too beautiful."

As if realizing how her remark might be taken, Felicity hurried to assure her cousin that she did not mean that *she* was not beautiful. "How could you not be, with your coal black hair and green eyes. Her Irish colleen, Aunt Anne used to call you. It is only—"

"Say no more," Regina said, "I understand perfectly. And you are correct in your assumption that no woman would employ someone of Constance's beauty. And if she did, your sister would not be safe in her employer's home. The gentlemen would be forever falling in love with her, and who can say how honorable would be their intentions."

"Exactly," Felicity agreed. "With her looks, the only logical thing for Constance is marriage."

Turning to stare at the fair beauty, Regina asked if she were betrothed.

"Of course she is not! Not that she has not had several offers, mind you. It is just that there are no eligible men in the neighborhood."

"At least none," the beauty added, "between the ages of sixteen and sixty."

"We had hoped," Felicity continued, "that when Constance came of age and was given her portion, we might journey to some place where she could be introduced into acceptable company. Not London, of course. We are not so foolish as to expect to mingle with exalted society. However, in some less formal setting, I do not doubt that Constance would have a dozen proposals within a month.''

Ignoring her sister's blushes at the unexpected compliment, Felicity all but shouted, ''Jupiter and Mars! Why did Father have to spend every last shilling?''

The question being unanswerable, the three young ladies fell silent, and only after the butler knocked at the door to ask if they would like a tea tray, did Constance return to the subject of Regina's future. ''Where will you go?''

Not certain how her cousins would react to her plans, Regina hesitated a moment before answering, pretending to savor the aroma of the steaming tea in her cup. ''Actually,'' she said, ''I am bound for Brighton on the morrow.''

''Brighton!'' the sisters exclaimed as one voice.

''Yes. I . . . I have a reason to believe that my father may live in the vicinity. I promised my mother that I would never give up searching for him, and now one of my letters of inquiry has been answered with information that a retired Colonel Farrington lives in a small village near Brighton. At least he did so as recently as two years ago.''

''Colonel?'' Constance asked. ''But your father was a lieutenant.''

''Try for a little wit,'' her sister advised. ''It has been twenty-seven years since Aunt Anne eloped with the young lieutenant. Soldiers do rise in rank, you know.''

Not in the least vexed by the reprimand, Constance persisted, asking her questions of her sister, almost as if their cousin were no longer in the room. ''But what if this man in Brighton proves to be some other Farrington? What will Gina do then? How will she live?"

Answering for herself, Regina said, "I have some money. Enough to sustain me for a while, at least."

Constance was apparently much struck by this information. "I had no idea that paid companions earned so much."

"As a rule, they do not."

"Then how can you afford—"

"Constance! Gina will be wishing she had not paid us this visit."

Regina felt the heat of embarrassment in her face. She had lived as an orphan for so long she had forgotten the give and take existing within a family, and the open inquisitiveness. But these two young women were, after all, her fleash and blood—possibly her only living relatives. "My wages were fifty pounds per annum," she said finally. "And if I were relying upon that money alone, I could not afford to go to Brighton.

"The thing is," she continued, "owing to the number of letters I wrote and received, I was obliged to inform Mrs. Phelps of my search for my father. You may imagine my surprise when her will was read, and I discovered that the dear old soul had left me five hundred pounds."

Felicity gasped. "Did you say, five *hundred?*"

"Yes. Her only stipulation was that I use the money to go to Brighton in person to meet this Colonel who might, or might not, be the man who eloped with my mother."

"But that is wonderful," Constance said. "I am happy for your good fortune, and I am certain Aunt Anne would be pleased to know—"

"That is it!" Felicity said, surprising her sister into

silence. "The perfect plan. I knew it was only a matter of time before I came up with an idea to save us."

Constance turned to stare hopefully at her younger sister. "You have thought of something? But how? What? Tell me quickly."

"It came to me right out of the blue, while Gina was talking. It is the answer to all our problems. Of course, we shall need Father's carriage, and we will be obliged to cajole John Coachman into driving, but other than that, we—"

"The berlin?" Her lovely eyes wide with curiosity, Constance said, "Why should we want that old thing? The springs are almost nonexistent and the roof leaks when it rains."

"Then I suggest," Felicity said, "that we pray for balmy weather, for arriving in our own carriage will lend us a certain respectability."

"Arriving where?"

"Why, Brighton, of course."

Regina had almost forgotten her young cousin's propensity for hatching schemes. When they were children, Felicity—though the youngest of the three—was forever dragging the other two into some adventure. Somehow, she had always been able to convince them that no harm would befall them; a statement that proved to be false more often than not.

"Felicity," Regina said, trepidation making her voice sound almost strident, "if memory serves me, the last of your schemes to which I was privy involved a lamb you were certain would make an excellent house pet."

"I remember that!" Constance said. "Only Felicity was too small to get the animal up the stairs to her bedchamber without our assistance, so—"

"So we gave in and helped her," Regina added. "Unfortunately, it was a kindness for which I, as the oldest, paid the dearest price."

Felicity giggled. "Who would have thought one wee lamb could leave so many little reminders of his presence in so many places?"

"Who, indeed? Even today I cannot look at a stair runner without recalling how long it took me to scrub those revolting spots off the carpet."

"I apologize most sincerely, Gina. But remember, I was but nine or ten years old at the time, and—"

"Do not, I beg you," Constance said, "accept age as a valid excuse." She looked at her sister. "Tell Gina how old you were when you gave one of the grooms sixpence to lend you the grass snake he kept in a box."

"A snake!" Regina could not help but shudder.

"It was for our mother's Aunt Sophie. She was visiting, and—"

"Miss Sophie Paxton? That disagreeable old prune who sipped sherry all day, then chewed cloves in an attempt to conceal the fact?"

"The very one," Felicity said.

"It was three years ago," Constance continued, "just after mother succumbed to the influenza, that Aunt Sophie came to Byrn Park for a visit. She had not been here above a sennight before she began hinting that Felicity and I were in need of a chaperone, and that for a small fee she would be willing to undertake the task. One had to feel sorry for the old girl, but—"

"I did not feel sorry for her!"

"That was obvious," Constance said, "for you dumped the grass snake in her bed."

Regina shuddered again. "I suppose the old prune screeched like an owl."

Constance shook her head. "She did not, though we listened well into the night. And the next day, when we stole up to her bedchamber, there was no sign of any restless tossing about in the bed. Nor, I regret to inform you, was there any sign of the snake."

Regina gasped. "Do not tell me it had excaped!"

It was Constance's turn to shudder. "I shall say only that I did not sleep for fully two months, for every time the sheet moved, I was certain the serpent had found its way to my room."

"What folly," Felicity said, "I am convinced that Aunt Sophie killed the creature and just never said anything about it."

The young lady's sister and cousin exchanged disgusted glances.

"Whatever you are planning this time, Felicity, allow me to inform you that—"

"Not to worry, Gina. We shall require but a month, perhaps less, and we will not interfere in any way with your conducting your search for Colonel Farrington. Further, I promise you we shall not infringe upon your time, nor inconvenience you in the slightest. You have my word on it."

The disclaimer had such a familiar ring to it that far from reassuring Regina, it had the opposite effect. "It will not serve. I am sorry to be disobliging, but—"

"If you are concerned about the money," the young lady said quietly, "you need have no fear on that score. We will pay you back every last farthing as soon as Constance is wed."

Regina had the grace to blush. "I am more than willing

to share my bequest with you. I hope you know that I would never leave the two of you to fend for yourselves. My disquiet is with this scheme to go to Brighton. It cannot work.''

"Why can it not?''

"Three young women alone?'' Regina said. "Believe me, we should be suspect the moment we set foot inside the town. Why, when I sent my request for lodging at a hotel, I was obliged to sign my letter *Mrs.* Farrington, representing myself as a widow who sought the medicinal benefits of sea bathing while eschewing all but the quietest of existences. If I had not done so, I never would have received a positive reply, for no respectable landlord would allow a lone, single woman inside his establishment.''

"But that is even better,'' Felicity said, not dissuaded, but rather encouraged by her cousin's venture into false representation. "Do you not see, to insure Constance's respectability, she will require a chaperone. Who better to fill the post than a widowed cousin?''

"But I am *not* widowed. Nor could I serve as anyone's chaperone. Though six and twenty may seem an advanced age to one who has only seventeen summers to her credit, you must take my word for it that others will not see it in the same light.''

"Pish,'' Felicity said, waving her hand as though brushing aside a pesky fly. "Do not be concerned on that score, for if we follow my plan, no one need ever know your true—''

"Furthermore,'' Regina said, not at all comfortable with her cousin's cavalier assumption that they would all fall in with her scheme, "what of Constance's feelings? Is she to throw herself away upon the first wealthy man who offers for her?''

The beauty shook her head. "Felicity would not wish me to wed a gentleman I took in great dislike. Nor would I accept the hand of anyone unwilling to open his home to her."

Impressed by this show of sisterly devotion, Regina felt herself weakening. "And what of you, Felicity? Will you seek a husband as well?"

"No. We have neither the time nor the money for launching more than one, and that one must be Constance. It will serve our purpose better if I find some way to make myself as nearly invisible as makes no difference."

"But that would be impossible. A charming girl like you, with your lively ways, must always be noticed."

"In this instance, I promise you I will not be. This opportunity to see Constance suitably wed is too important, so whatever is required of me, that I will do."

She came forward then and caught both Regina's hands, squeezing them tightly and looking up at her in a straightforward, yet beseeching way that her cousin found difficult to resist. "Ask any task of me, Gina, and I will do it. Only say you will take us to Brighton with you. Please."

Regina wanted to say her nay, but as she looked into the pixie face, the words would not form upon her lips. "This is sheer lunacy," she said. "It will never work."

"Oh, Gina," Felicity squealed, throwing her arms around her cousin's waist. "You are so good."

"But I did not say I had agreed. I only said—"

Felicity hugged her tightly. "You will not regret this, Gina. I promise."

After two hectic days spent planning strategy, packing such clothes as would be needed by the participants, and practicing the story agreed upon as the most likely to be accepted by Brighton society, the three cousins bid farewell forever to Byrn Park, their destination the seashore. Also joining them in their escapade was a hard-working girl of eighteen who had filled the role of chambermaid for the sisters for the last three years. The maid, Bessie, had begged to be allowed to come with them.

"Please take me, Miss Felicity. I've no wish to stay behind to serve a new mistress. 'Specially not when I could be seeing the sights of Brighton."

Felicity, in complete charity with such sentiment, readily agreed that a servant would only add to their consequence, and since Regina had given up arguing as a lost cause, the maid was added to their party.

So it was that on Wednesday, June fifth, an ancient berlin driven by a country-bred coachman joined the constant stream of traffic on the London to Brighton road. Within slightly less than three hours, the briny smell of the sea greeted the passengers of the ill-sprung coach, and several minutes later they were treated to their first view of the famous watering place.

Awed by the whiteness of the buildings, as well as the throng of pedestrians who strolled along the Steine, the young ladies stared wide-eyed, their mouths agape, especially when the coachman drove past the Prince Regent's Chinese Pavilion with its onion dome and minarets. Nor did the *oohs* and *ahs* lessen when John Coachman turned the horses onto West Cliff and continued past the fashionable Old Ship Inn. The country misses were still chattering with delight when the team was reined in before an unpretentious, cobble-fronted family hotel called The Knight's Arms.

While the three younger members of the party vied for

a place at the far window of the coach, eager for their first glimpse of the waters of the Channel—waters that lapped gently against the shingled beach—Regina allowed the porter to hand her down to the street.

"Mrs. Farrington?" inquired the landlord, a short, stick-thin man who had lost no time in presenting himself at the brick-trimmed entrance.

"I am Mrs. Farrington," she replied, wishing she dared lift the heavy black veil that all but obscured her vision. Infusing her voice with as much authority as she could muster, she said, "You are the landlord, I presume."

"Yardley, madam. At your service. If you will please to follow me, I shall—"

"Come along," she called to the three females still inside the coach, and though her sight was hampered by the veil, she was well able to see the surprise on the landlord's face when the abigail tumbled from the coach, followed by a schoolroom chit of perhaps fourteen, her beribboned braids bouncing about her shoulders.

"Madam," Mr. Yardley said, the warmth gone from his voice, "I understood from your letter that you would be traveling alone."

"My plans changed. As you see, I am not alone, and for that reason I shall require a suite with two bedrooms."

"But, madam, at this time of year we are booked well in advance, and—"

"I was informed," she replied with what she hoped was an air of command, "that your hotel would be able to extend to me all the courtesies necessary to my comfort. In fact, I quite depended upon it."

"The maid will be no problem, of course, madam, for there are attic rooms for those servants traveling with their employers, but I am not certain we can accommodate an added guest. That is, we cannot do so unless you are willing to share your bedchamber with the young lady. In that instance . . ."

Regina was about to inform him once again that a second bedchamber was required when Constance emerged from the coach, stepping down to the street and making further conversation unnecessary. At the sight of the fair beauty, her perfect features displayed to a nicety by a wide-poked bonnet of azure blue, Mr. Yardley seemed to lose his train of thought. As he stared, his mouth fell open while his already protuberant eyes threatened to pop from his head, and only after a concerted effort was he able to recall himself to his duties.

"Please," he said, gazing bemusedly at the young lady, "won't you come this way."

After Regina signed the gilt-edged visitor's registry at the manager's desk, the three cousins and Betsy were shown up a broad staircase to the suite. Since none of the four country misses had ever spent so much as a single night in a public establishment, they found nothing to dislike in the accommodations.

The parlor, though not large, was pleasantly furnished with a pair of gold brocade bergere chairs, a bombe chest, and a loo table with accompanying cane-back chairs. As well, companion settees and pembroke tables were arranged on either side of the fireplace. The highlight of the room was, of course, the view. From either of the two tall windows, one could see the busy street out front, the rough cliff's edge just beyond, and farther out, the gray, easy rolling waves of the sea.

"Look!" Felicity said, kneeling on the window seat and

letting down the sash so that fresh, moist air blew into the room, "there is the Channel. The first thing I will do is set up my telescope."

While Felicity made good her promise, quickly loosening the straps of the leather carrying case and withdrawing the tripod upon which the telescope would stand, Regina motioned Constance toward the two bedchambers. "Whichever room is largest, choose that for you and Felicity."

"Oh, no. Really, Gina, you must take the larger chamber. After all, it is you who are paying for everything."

"Please. Let us hear no more upon that subject."

Constance, perceiving the flush that stained her cousin's cheeks, vowed not to mention money again. Their cousin had been kindness itself to share her good fortune with them, in fact, if she had not, Constance truly had no idea what would have become of them. However, if Gina found their words of gratitude uncomfortable, Constance saw no point in embarrassing her further.

She knew that the best way to show her gratitude was to find a suitable parti as quickly as possible so that she and her sister might be as little drain as possible on Gina's finances, yet Constance found the thought more daunting than she dared admit to anyone. Not that she had anything against the wedded state. Actually, nothing could be further from the truth. She wanted a home and a husband, it was just . . . Tears stung the back of her throat, and she was obliged to swallow several times to keep the sobs at bay. It was just that she so wanted to marry for love.

Her Aunt Anne had married a man she loved, and all her life Constance had been warned by her father to see where such folly led.

"Abandonment and misery are my sister's lot," Papa

would always say, "and save for my generosity, she and her brat would be residing in the poor house."

Of course, Constance's mother had thought *she* was making a good marriage, and if there was ever a miserable lady, it was Sir Hubert Mitchell's wife! Of the two sisters-in-law, Constance thought she much preferred her aunt's fate; if nothing else, Aunt Anne loved her husband to her dying day.

"I have an idea," Felicity said to the room at large. "What say you to our leaving the mundane task of unpacking until later? I, for one, believe we should spend our first few hours in Brighton in frivolous pursuits."

Constance, not wanting to think about the possibility that she might never know the thrill of romantic love, was more than happy to fall in with her sister's suggestion. Gina was a bit less enthusiastic about an excursion, but that was only because she was obliged to wear her widow's garb. And who could fault her for detesting the unrelieved black dress and the nearly opaque veil?

"Please," Felicity said, looking to Gina, "once Constance begins accepting invitations, you will be needed to act as her chaperone, and I shall probably not leave the suite from one day to the next."

Since Betsy, too, turned upon their benefactress a look reminiscent of a dog who had never had a full meal in its entire life—a look only a stone heart could have ignored—it was not to be marvelled at that Gina's capitulation was swift. Never mind that the Widow Farrington had checked into the Knight's Arms for the avowed purpose of recuperating her strength, in less than ten minutes following her arrival, she and her two charges, escorted by their abigail, descended the staircase at an enthusiastic pace.

With a great deal of feminine chatter, the quartet exited

the building, turned to their left, and hurried off in the direction of the Marine Parade. Frivolous their pursuit might have been, but no one enjoyed it more than Regina. After five years spent as companion to an elderly lady, the activity and noise were exciting. The cries of the sea birds circling and diving out over the water, the muted crashing of the surf as it rushed to meet the shingled beach, the snatches of conversation of the dozens of beautifully dressed couples who strolled the famous promenade—all were music to Regina's ears.

No less than her companions did she look her fill of the famous watering place, enjoying the novelty of the sights, the sounds, and the salty breeze.

"There are the bathing machines," Felicity informed them, pointing to several small, brightly painted wooden huts. Equipped with wheels, the machines were drawn into the Channel by horses until their floors were level with the water, at which time, the bather—in this instance a brave female, completely covered in a flannel bathing costume and gauze worsted stockings—emerged to be dipped in the sea water by a professional bathing woman.

Though Constance shuddered at the thought of actually being in that vast expanse of water, Felicity breathed an awed sigh. "Before we leave," said the irrepressible young lady, I want to try sea bathing. I know I should enjoy the experience prodigiously."

"Like as not," Betsy said, pointing toward the beach where a half dozen young males held spy glasses to their eyes, "them gentlemen would enjoy it prodigiously too. Just look at 'em, ogling that lady bather, while the wet flannel clings to her like a second skin."

"Scandalous!" said a middle-aged gentleman who happened to be passing by. Lifting his hat in greeting, he

sketched them a bow that caused his stays to creak. Since
he was a complete stranger to them, and had the effrontery
to ogle Constance in much the same manner as those
rogues on the beach had ogled the bather, Regina saw no
reason to afford him the least civility.

"Come," she said, turning her back to the man, "let us
continue our walk."

As they left the man behind, Gina stole a look at Constance. Her cousin looked straight ahead, but her lovely
face was pale, and she held her handkerchief to her lips,
as if she might be unwell.

As they passed one of the two subscription libraries on
the Steine, another unknown gentleman lifted his hat to
Constance, while another peered at her through his quiz-
zing glass. Deciding her cousin had endured enough
embarrassment, Gina suggested they forego the Prince
Regent's Royal Pavilion, their previously agreed upon destination, and return to the inn. "I have had my fill of looking
and being looked at for one day."

Not even Felicity objected to the change in plans, for
she had not been unaware of her sister's discomfort. And
no wonder, for the place seemed to be peopled by middle-
aged roues—all of them old enough to be her father, and
a few of them corpulent enough to resemble His Royal
Highness. It was not at all unusual for gentlemen to be
interested in Constance, but where were the gentlemen
who were likely to interest her? Where were the *young* men?

Feeling as though she had been duped into believing
Brighton a place where a lady might form an eligible connection, Felicity was more than ready to retrace her steps.
Unaccustomed to such crowded streets, she did not expect
someone to be just behind her, and as she turned, she
collided with a young gentleman carrying an armload of

books. Felicity might have fallen if the gentleman had not abandoned his books and caught her by the elbows, holding her steady until she regained her balance.

"Oh," she said, rather breathlessly, looking up into the pleasant face of a red-haired gentleman some three or four years her senior. "Your pardon, sir."

"No, no, I should have been watching where I trod. Are you hurt, little one?"

Little one? For a moment she had forgotten that she wore the short dress and pinafore of a child.

Constance was the first of the party to step forward. "Thank you for your quickness, sir. You saved my sister from a nasty fall."

"Not at all, ma'am, I—"

The young man stopped mid-sentence, obviously only just noticing the blond beauty. After staring at her for several seconds, looking as bemused as if he had been dealt a telling blow from some flying object, he suddenly recalled his manners and snatched the curly-brimmed beaver from his head. "It was my pleasure, ma'am."

"May I offer my gratitude as well," Regina said, offering him her hand. "This is our first day in Brighton, and it would have been a pity to begin it with an accident. Thank you, Mr. . . ."

"Drayson, ma'am. Oliver Drayson."

While the Mitchell sisters became acquainted with the delights of Brighton, and Brighton became acquainted with the exquisite beauty of Constance Mitchell, a gentleman on the opposite side of the county, near the little village of Chiveley, pondered a letter handed to him only moments earlier by his valet.

"Not bad news, I trust, m'lord."

Joel Harcourt, the sixth baron Harcourt, crossed the
richly patterned Axminster carpet that covered his bedchamber floor and plopped down in a plain oak corner
chair. It being the third Monday of the month, his lordship
had spent the entire day riding over the rolling hills and
slowly ripening fields of his estate. Because of the unseason-
ably cool weather, he had chosen to visit each of his tenants
in turn, assuring himself that everyone was in good health
and that the cottages were in good repair.

As a result of that ride, his thick, tobacco-brown hair
was thoroughly windblown, his bottle-green coat and once-
crisp neckcloth were rumpled, and his Hessians and panta-
loons were liberally splattered with mud. While absently
raising first one foot then the other so the servant could
remove the offending boots, he read through his letter a
second time.

My Dear Nephew,
   *I am at my wit's end, and if you do not come to my
rescue, I do not know what I shall do. It is your cousin.
He has found more to like here in Brighton than the salubrious air. He fancies himself in love! And with a Circe whose
background and connections are shrouded in mystery.*
   *Oliver will not listen to reason regarding this female, and
I cannot go to her myself to beg her to break it off with my
boy, for I have had a stupid accident and broken my toe.*
   *Please come to Brighton as soon as possible. If you hold
me in any regard at all, you will not delay.*
                              Your loving aunt, Beatrix

Joel rubbed his hand across his chin, ignoring the
scraping sound of a full-day's growth of beard as he tried

to picture his young cousin in the throes of love. A studious young man still several months short of his majority, Oliver Drayson had never shown the least interest in the young ladies of the neighborhood. In fact, his overriding passion was science, and until the arrival of this letter, Joel had thought the lad immune to the charms of the fair sex.

The mysterious female must be a siren indeed!

Naturally, Joel would go. He liked the boy too much to stand by and let him become entangled in the web of some adventuress. Furthermore, he was excessively fond of his aunt. She was his father's sister, and since the death of his parents, she and Oliver were his only remaining relatives.

That they were in Brighton was unfortunate. Joel despised the place; especially in June and July when the Prince Regent and his set swelled the boundaries of the once-charming little seaside town.

Not altogether pleased with the summons, yet unwilling to ignore it, Joel crumpled the letter and tossed it onto the leather-topped writing table to his left. "We shall be traveling to Brighton tomorrow," he informed his valet. "My aunt, Mrs. Drayson, needs me."

Chapter Two

It was late afternoon of the following day before Lord Harcourt arrived in Brighton and presented himself at his aunt's rented residence in the Royal Crescent. Jumping down from his curricle and tossing the reins of the well-matched bays to the groom, Joel stepped up to the door of the second of a row of white stuccoed houses that stood on the cliff top facing the sea.

All was quiet on the elegant street where leisure was the sole occupation; while in the blue distance beyond the shoreline, birds of all sizes and colors soared above the gray waters of the channel, their calls a constant reminder of their day-to-day search for food.

As Joel lifted the knocker, then waited for admittance, assured of his welcome, he watched dozens of black-backed gulls circling in chains as they floated aloft. Again and again they issued their loud, rough *kac, kac, kac* to warn off the agile, golden-crowned gannets, for the gannets skimmed along the sea in a steady sailing manner, threatening to capture all the likeliest morsels.

"Good afternoon, sir," said the very proper butler who opened the door. Hired with the house, the servant did not recognize the visitor. "May I help you?"

Reminded of his purpose for calling upon his aunt, Joel abandoned his contemplation of the sea and the ever-busy fowl and presented his visiting card. "I am Lord Harcourt. Mrs. Drayson is expecting me."

Bowing respectfully, the butler took Joel's hat and gloves then led him up to the small withdrawing room on the first floor, announcing him to the plump, middle-aged lady who lounged upon a rose brocade couch, her bound foot resting upon a small needlepoint footstool.

"Joel, my dear boy," Mrs. Beatrix Drayson cried. "You have come at last."

Politely refraining from informing his relative that her letter had only just arrived the day before, Joel saluted the injured lady's cheek. "You are looking well, Aunt Trixie. The sea air seems to have worked its magic, assisting you in your recuperation from the influenza."

"Yes," she replied, "I am quite recovered."

"I am happy to hear it, ma'am. And if I may, allow me to congratulate you as well upon that cap. My compliments," he said, indicating the bit of lace and ribbon pinned atop his aunt's salt and pepper curls. "Quite fetching."

"La, Harcourt, you always know the very thing to say to make a woman forget what she is about. Which is exactly why I sent for you. I knew you were the very man for the job."

"Job, Aunt?"

"Yes," replied the lady, motioning for her visitor to take

the seat opposite her couch, "for you have your work cut out for you."

Disposing himself upon a lyre-back chair, Joel stretched his long legs out in front of him in a relaxed manner. "Am I to assume the situation has grown more serious?"

"Serious? My boy, matters have come to a dangerous point. You will find this difficult to credit, but last evening Oliver asked me—ever so casually, mind you—how long it had been since the Drayson betrothal ring had been seen by a jeweler."

At this news, Joel sat up straight, all semblance of relaxation gone. "Drat the lad! What has gotten into him?"

"Infatuation," replied his aunt. "I refuse to dignify the passion by calling it love. My son is bewitched. Quite beyond the reach of reason."

"And the young woman? What do you know of her? Is she of the muslin company, do you think?"

At this, his aunt shook her head. "I only wish it were so, for I should know how to deal with such a creature. Regrettably, this female—Miss Constance Mitchell, she calls herself—has all the appearance of a gently reared young lady. And though her arrival in Brighton was unexceptionable—with a chaperone, a little sister, and a servant in tow—there is about the entire group a certain havey-cavey air."

"How so, Aunt?"

"It is almost as though they are all players acting their parts. Not that I have anything specific upon which to base my suspicions, you understand. Nothing save a mother's intuition where her child's welfare is concerned."

"I see."

Joel was inclined to give heed to his aunt's intuition, for unlike many women with only one offspring, Beatrix

Drayson had never been the kind of parent who imposed her fears upon her son. She had always allowed Oliver as much freedom as possible to explore new ideas and occupations, never smothering him with unwanted attention.

"Baseless or not, Aunt Trixie, what is your strongest suspicion about this girl?"

"I suspect that she is impoverished and has come to Brighton for no other purpose than to catch a wealthy husband. And considering some of the rather loose fish who number among her admirers, I cannot think she is at all particular about the age or reputation of her future partner. That being so, I am ready to take my stand against Heaven and Earth to insure that my son is not her final choice."

Joel could not refrain from smiling at this impassioned speech. "When taking a stand against any adversary, Aunt, a broken toe is not an asset."

"As you say," his relative concurred. "That is why I quite depend upon you in this, my hour of need."

After agreeing to find out all he could about his cousin's inamorata, and to protect the lad from being taken in if the girl should prove to be an adventuress, Joel asked where he might find the Mitchell entourage.

"They are staying at The Knight's Arms, a respectable enough inn, though not of the first stare, but I believe you may find them this afternoon at the new rooms at the Castle Inn. Oliver mentioned something about a German string quartet performing there—selections from Bach, he said—and since my son is noted for his tin ear, and is as ignorant of one composer as he is the next, I can only assume that Miss Mitchell meant to attend the concert."

* * *

Acting upon his aunt's suggestion, Lord Harcourt drove straight away to the northwest corner of the Steine and Castle Square, the site of the Castle Inn. Pausing only long enough to pay his subscription and sign his name in the book, he declined the offer made by Mr. Firth, the master of ceremonies, to introduce him to some of the other subscribers. "I believe my cousin, Mr. Oliver Drayson, is here."

"So he is, my lord. In the company of Mrs. Farrington and Miss Mitchell. Shall I help you find his party?"

Declining that offer as well, Joel chose instead to stroll into the first of the suite of simple yet elegant rooms. The string quartet had only just completed its performance, and following the polite applause, waiters had begun to scurry about the room, their trays laden with pots of steaming tea and little baskets of sugar cakes.

A quick perusal of the room revealed Mr. Oliver Drayson seated at a small table quite near one of the many paintings of Cupid and Psyche. Sitting opposite him was a lady rigged out in the somber black of widowhood. Nineteen or ninety, her age was difficult to estimate because the heavy widow's veil that covered her from her head to her hips rendered her virtually featureless. Logic said the widow must be the chaperone, for to his cousin's left, her back to Joel, sat a trim-figured female dressed in an azure blue pelisse and a matching wide-poked bonnet.

Miss Constance Mitchell, Joel presumed.

He studied his cousin who was still four months shy of his twenty-first birthday. A thoroughly likeable young man, Oliver was the image of his deceased father, Sir Lindford Drayson. Though quite slender, the lad had come to terms with his slight build and the fact that he was several inches shorter than his cousin Joel's six feet, but he was still at war with the fates for having given him his father's carrot-colored hair.

It was the unfortunate hair, coupled with the lad's penchant for all things scientific, especially astronomy, that had made him a bit shy in company. What, Joel wondered, could have induced his cousin to overcome his shyness?

The answer was not long in coming, for as Joel strolled leisurely across the room, the young lady in blue chanced to drop her reticule, and when she bent to retrieve the small beaded bag, Joel stepped forward.

"Allow me," he said.

Bending one knee to the floor, he scooped up the reticule, then as he handed it over to its owner, he lifted his gaze to the face beneath the blue bonnet. For just a moment, he was rendered speechless. The face was that of an angel. A blue-eyed, golden-haired angel.

No less mortal than the next man, Joel stared unashamedly at the beauty. He could not help himself. Here was a true diamond of the first water, and from the artless blush that stained her alabaster cheeks, the young lady was either an innocent as yet unjaded by masculine attention, or she was a consummate actress.

Unfortunately, those few brief moments were not enough to allow him to discover which estimate was nearer the truth.

"Harcourt!"

Recalled to his mission by his cousin's surprised voice, Joel rose to confront Mr. Drayson.

"Well met, Oliver," he said, extending his hand in greeting. "I have only just come from a visit with my aunt in the Royal Crescent. It was she who informed me that I might find you here."

Obviously suspicious of his cousin's sudden appearance, Mr. Drayson did not immediately take Joel's proffered hand. "Why are you here?" he asked. his tone decidedly belligerent.

"Why?" Joel repeated, lifting one eyebrow. "Why not? It is June. The warm sea beckons. And all the world and his wife are come to Brighton." He put his hand on the younger man's shoulder. "Am I not welcome, Cousin?" he asked softly.

Oliver's face turned the color of his hair. "Your pardon, sir. I . . . that is . . ."

Never one to engage in uneven sparring, Joel said, "Will you make me known to your friends?"

"Of course," Oliver replied. "Mrs. Farrington," he said, speaking to the person obscured by the veil, "may I present my cousin, Lord Harcourt?"

"How do you do, Lord Harcourt," said a voice whose owner might have been anything from nineteen to ninety.

Curious, Joel tried to see the face beneath the heavy silk. It was like attempting to read a newspaper while in a darkened room. "An honor, Mrs. Farrington," he said politely.

"And this is Mrs. Farrington's cousin, Miss Constance Mitchell."

Joel bowed to the angel in blue. "Your servant, Miss Mitchell. Since I have it on good authority that Oliver is not musical, may I assume that you are the devotee of Bach?"

Apparently no more knowledgeable on the subject of composers than was Mr. Drayson, the young lady blinked her dark, thick eyelashes. "Bach?"

It was the female beneath the veil who came to the chit's rescue. "I am the guilty party, my lord."

"Gulity, ma'am?"

"The devotee," she corrected, a touch of annoyance in her voice.

Intrigued to discover that the voice was considerably younger than ninety, and curious to know how much younger, Joel directed his next question to the chaperone. "Did the string quartet perform to your satisfaction, ma'am?"

Her face shielded from view, Regina bit her lip. *Drat the man! First he tries to pierce the armor of my veil, and now he is attempting to draw me out.*

She had made it a practice this past fortnight to speak as little as possible while in company, lest someone suspect she was not the elderly widow she pretended to be. For the most part, the ploy had succeeded, principally because the gentlemen had not been able to tear their attention from the beautiful Constance.

When they first began this charade, Regina had supposed that everyone who met her must immediately see through her disguise; she had expected to be exposed as a fraud within the first few minutes. To her surprise, no one she met even lifted an eyebrow. Though, in all honesty, she should not have been all that surprised, for it was a sad commentary upon their times that a marriageable female was judged in the main upon her youth and beauty. Without those two attributes, or the palliative of a handsome dowry, a lady soon faded into the background, unnoticed and unremarked. As for a spinster past a certain age, that pitiable creature was virtually invisible.

Now, after nearly three weeks of going about unnoticed, Regina had uttered an unguarded word and called attention to herself. In an attempt to keep Mr. Drayson's cousin from asking questions of Constance that would show her in a bad light, Regina had laid herself open to a catechism that could reveal *her* as an imposter.

With no recourse but to brave it out, she said, "I should be hard to please, Lord Harcourt, if I found fault with the musicians, for they are famous throughout Europe. I believe they performed at one of the recent celebrations in honor of the wedding of Princess Charlotte and Prince Leopold."

"High praise indeed," he said.

Regina could not discern if the newcomer was being sarcastic or sincere, but something in his manner put her on her guard. Of a certainty, Mr. Drayson was acting wary. The young man had been surprised to see his cousin; in fact, he had been less than pleased with the encounter. Did he suspect that Mrs. Drayson had sent Lord Harcourt to see what he could discover about Constance? It was a distinct possibility.

Of course, Mr. Drayson's reaction might be no more than fear of competition for Constance's attention. Not that there were not usually a number of gentlemen vying for her notice. However, Lord Harcourt was of a different stamp altogether from the majority of her cousin's admirers.

With the exception of Mr. Oliver Drayson, who was a most gentlemanly young man, Regina had found little to like in the dozen or so males who had called upon Constance, bringing her bouquets and soliciting her company for walks along the Marine Parade. To Regina, those other men seemed a rather rackety bunch—a bit jaded, and far too free with their compliments—and she had begun to fear that Felicity's matrimonial scheme for her beautiful sister was destined to fail.

With Lord Harcourt's arrival, however, Regina felt encouraged. If his reasons for coming to Brighton were as he had stated them—merely a wish for salubrious air and pleasant company—then here was a gentleman worthy of Constance's notice. In addition to being older than his cousin, and a member of the peerage, he also displayed an air of refinement lacking in the other admirers. And if the exquisite cut of his clothes was anything to go by, he was also quite wealthy, a fact that rendered Lord Harcourt in every way a desirable parti.

Tall and broad shouldered, with the physique of an athlete, there was about him a look of health, as though he spent a good deal of time out of doors in the fresh air, rather than in the smoke-filled gaming hells of London.

As different from those dissipated men of the Prince Regent's set as day was from night, Lord Harcourt fairly exuded vitality. And he was handsome enough to capture any female's heart. Stealing a glance at his thick, dark hair and his angular face, Regina felt her own pulse quicken.

Pure foolishness on her part, of course. Paid companions of six and twenty, if they were wise, did not commit the folly of allowing their thoughts to dwell overlong on such men. The Lord Harcourts of this world could pick and choose where they wished, and it was a fact of life that they never chose portionless females well past their first blush of youth.

"May I join you?" he asked.

Some survival instinct told Regina she should refuse him, but unable to do so, she indicated the vacant chair to her left.

With a smile that should have warned her of his intentions, Lord Harcourt pulled out the chair, lifting it easily, and placing it at an angle to the small table, closer to Regina than was necessary.

"Tea?" she asked nervously, touching the handle of the small crockery tea pot.

"I thank you, no. Actually, I should much rather spend these few moments getting to know more about you and the lovely Miss Mitchell."

"A few moments," Regina repeated hopefully. "Are you promised elsewhere, sir? If so, we would not wish to detain you."

She thought she detected a slight pull at the corners of his mouth, as though he were trying to hide his amusement at her discomfort. "You are very kind, ma'am, to be so solicitous of my time. Aside from my cousin, however, I have no particular friends in Brighton, and no obligations whatsoever. I am, as the saying goes, free as the birds of the air. I can fly away whenever I wish. Or," he added, leaning rather close to her and lowering his voice, "I can remain as long as it pleases me."

Regina swallowed with diffculty, for his last remark sounded awfully like a threat. "H-how delightful, sir."

"My condolences upon your bereavement," he said, surprising her with the change of subject.

"Thank you, sir, I—"

"How long have you been a widow?"

Taken aback by the abrupt question, Regina affected a bout of coughing to give her time to form an answer. Never comfortable with falsehoods in general, and most particularly afraid she might get tripped up by a piece of forgotten fiction while here in Brighton, she had vowed to adhere to the truth as much as possible. "How long, sir? *Long* is a relative term, surely, for the measurement of time has much to do with the person involved."

"Mere semantics," he said, giving her a look that said he was ready for a battle of words if that was her weapon of choice. "I consider time an absolute, so you must explain to me how it is that people influence its measurement."

"For instance, sir, think of a child awaiting an approaching birthday. Such a youngster might find a week an eternity; whereas a woman happy in her marriage might deem thirty years but a fleeting moment."

"And were you such a woman?" he asked, his tone implying that he already doubted her answer.

Not wanting to reply to that question, she returned to his original one regarding the length of time she had been a widow, giving an answer that was both evasive and truthful. "I donned my mourning clothes but recently, sir. Now, if you will forgive me, I do not wish to speak of this matter further."

As a gentleman, he had no recourse but to abandon the subject. Unfortunately, good manners did not dissuade him from introducing other topics. "Miss Mitchell is a very beautiful young lady," he said.

Though Regina felt on safer ground here, she exhaled loudly enough to rustle the heavy veil. "Constance is quite lovely. Both in appearance and in character."

Lord Harcourt inclined his head as if acknowledging a point scored to Regina. "Puzzling, is it not, that her family did not see fit to send such a beauty to town for a season?"

"To understand that particular circumstance, one must know the lady's father. Sir Hubert was interested in many things; unfortunately, the list of his concerns did not include either of his daughters. Both Constance and her younger sister were left to twiddle their thumbs at Byrn

Park, with no thought given to their futures. Only since Sir Hubert's demise have the girls been free to see a bit of the countryside. Hence this trip to the seashore.''

"Byrn Park, you say?"

"Yes. Their home is near the Kent border, about three miles west of the village of Burwish. The estate is, of course, entailed upon a male heir, so the new baronet is a distant relation. However,'' Regina added, an edge to her voice that she did not try to conceal, ''if you should wish to know more concerning my cousins, anyone in the neighborhood can supply you with information.''

Lord Harcourt's expression was unreadable, but he stood and made her a bow—albeit an abbreviated one. "If I have given offense, madam, pray accept my apologies. I had no wish to do so.''

"You had no wish to give offense?" she asked, "or no wish to apologize?"

For just a moment he stared at her, then his lips twitched at the corners. "Semantics again, Mrs. Farrington?"

"Syntax,'' she corrected. "Misplaced modifiers, I believe.''

This time he laughed aloud. "If we should meet again, ma'am, I shall be on my guard at all times.''

"And I will do likewise, my lord. If we should meet again.''

Chapter Three

"How old is Mr. Drayson's cousin?" Felicity asked, her pixie's face quite animated with interest. "Was he handsome? Did he show any partiality for Constance?" Not waiting for the answers, she moved away from the second-floor window and the telescope she had focused on a pair of sailing boats out on the Channel. "How frustrating it is to be obliged to remain behind here in the suite, not partaking of any but the most innocuous of outings."

"You chose your own role," Regina said, motioning toward the school-girl ensemble of shin-length pink dress, white lawn fichu, and wide satin sash tied into a bow at the back.

Felicity groaned. "If you have any affection for me, Gina, do not, I beg of you, remind me of my folly. How was I to know I would be barred, like the veriest child, from all the most interesting activities of the town?"

Removing the detested veil, Regina held it toward her

young cousin. "Perhaps we could exchange places. You may be the chaperone for a time while I remain at the inn. Believe me, I should be more than happy to quit my part in this charade."

Immediately Regina regretted her waspish retort. It was not Felicity's fault that Lord Harcourt had angered her with his interrogation. Nor was her cousin culpable for the elusive Mr. Thom Newton's continued absence from his little pigeonhole of an office on the corner of North Street.

"Forgive me," Regina said. "I am blue deviled because I still have not had my interview with Mr. Newton. We have been in town for a fortnight, and I am no closer to finding my father than I was before we arrived."

"I am sorry," Felicity said softly. Then, rather shyly, "Is that all that is plaguing you?"

"Whatever do you—?"

"Is it money? I know this suite is expensive. Far more costly than any of us had expected it would be. I wish you will tell me, please, is the money disappearing very fast?"

Not wanting to discuss the matter, nor to consider what might happen if her funds ran out before she found her father, Regina tossed the veil on the round loo table, disposed herself upon one of the walnut Windsor chairs, and addressed the easiest of her cousin's previous questions. "You asked about Lord Harcourt's age."

"Yes," Felicity said.

Obviously taking her cue from Regina that she did not wish to discuss finances, the young lady took the chair opposite her cousin and leaned her elbows upon the table. "Is he much older than Mr. Drayson?"

"Bearing in mind that one cannot be certain of anything when obliged to view a gentleman through a silk haze, I

should estimate Lord Harcourt to be about thirty or thirty-
one.''

"So old?'' How disappointing.''

"Old!'' Regina almost choked on the word. "Lord Harcourt is in his prime. Furthermore, he is the first gentleman
we have met who fulfills your requirements for Constance's
future husband.''

"How can you say so?'' Felicity asked rather vehemently.
"Have you forgotten Mr. Drayson?''

"No, but—''

"Surely *he* is everything that is admirable in a gentleman.''

"True,'' Regina replied, not missing the crimson that
stained the young lady's cheeks or the passion in her voice.
"But you must allow that Mr. Drayson has one undeniable
drawback.''

Felicity's gray eyes flashed with indignation. "I do not
see that! He is of good family, and soon he will inherit
his—''

"Soon," Regina repeated. "At the moment he is but
twenty years old. Should he wish to marry, he must either
wait for his birthday, or he must apply to his mama for
consent to wed.''

"Oh.''

"Oh, indeed.''

Not willing to introduce a subject that would only add
to her cousin's discomfort, Regina refrained from giving
voice to her present thoughts. Nonetheless, she could not
help but wonder what might have happened if they had
come to Brighton under different circumstances—each in
her own *persona*. If that had been the case, and if she
read Mr. Drayson's character and interests correctly, the

gentleman might more logically have centered his attention upon Felicity rather than her sister.

Not free to introduce such conjectures, however, Regina remained silent. It was just as well, for at that moment a knock sounded at the door. When Felicity answered the summons, the porter presented her with a floral tribute containing two dozen red roses wrapped about with silver paper.

Her arms filled, the young lady returned to the table. "Mmm," she said, breathing deeply of the sweet aroma. "I wonder which of Constance's admirers sent these beauties?"

After searching among the blossoms for a card, she finally found the white square of pasteboard. "It is from Lord Harcourt. Whatever his age," she said, "one must at least admire his choice of flowers."

Turning the card over, she read the words written on the reverse. "Semantics. Syntax. A rose by any other name would smell as sweet."

She looked questioningly at Regina. "What can it mean?"

Unwilling to give voice to an outright falsehood, Regina merely shook her head.

"Is it a conundrum, do you suppose? If it is, it will not serve, for Constance will not know the answer. She is never successful at riddles." Felicity read the message through again. "Whatever its meaning, I vow 'tis a most unloverlike message."

Regina was not nearly so discriminating as her young cousin, and she felt her entire body grow warm with emotion. It required a concerted effort for her not to reach out and take the card. The roses were for her! In twenty-six years she had never received a single flower; now here were two dozen of natures most beautiful blossoms.

Were they meant as an apology? She decided they must be. Of a certainty they were not meant as a tribute, for she had never heard that eligible gentlemen made a practice of sending that most romantic of flowers to females believed to be middle-aged widows.

"Be so good as to put them in water," she instructed Felicity.

While her cousin searched through the bombe chest for a vase large enough to accommodate the bouquet, Regina carefully removed a single rose and took it to her bedchamber. Closing the door behind her, she leaned against the wood, and with her eyes closed, she breathed deeply of the flower's heavenly fragrance. If Lord Harcourt's ruggedly handsome face intruded upon her thoughts, bringing with it a sudden acceleration in the rhythm of her heart, Regina supposed that was no more than should be expected.

"I wish I had been able to see the color of his eyes," she whispered.

After a time, she strode over to the dresser and picked up a small book of Shakespearean sonnets she had purchased only the day before at The Royal Marine Library. Carefully placing the rose between the middle most pages, she closed the book and put it in the top drawer of the dresser, taking care that none of it showed beneath the stack of freshly laundered handkerchiefs.

Midmorning of the next day Joel left the Old Ship Inn where he had procured a room and strolled purposefully westward toward The Knight's Arms. It was his intention to wait upon Miss Constance Mitchell at the inn, for after reflecting upon his encounter the day before with the young lady and her mysterious chaperone, he was convinced that his aunt's intuition regarding those two was correct. They were most definitely playing a part, and he meant to discover what they had in mind for his unsuspecting cousin.

Joel was still some distance from the cobble-fronted entrance to The Knight's Arms when fate played into his hands. To his surprise, a veiled figure emerged from the inn. The figure was none other than the alleged Mrs. Farrington, and on the instant Joel knew he must follow her.

The mysterious lady looked first to her left then to her right, though how she could see anything through that thick veil, one could only guess. Obviously satisfied that she was not being observed, she proceeded westward. At the corner she turned to her right, continuing up West Street, which had once been the western-most of the four boundaries of the old fishing village of Brightelmstone.

She traversed West Street for some little way, walking quickly, as though hurrying to keep an appointment, and since she never looked back, Joel was able to follow her rather closely without fear of detection. When she reached the corner of North Street, she knocked at the door of a small office, then she disappeared inside the rather seedy-looking establishment.

What on earth could she want in such a place?

Joel had not long to ponder the question. Whatever she wanted, she obviously had not gotten it, for within little more than a minute she was outside again, slamming the door angrily before retracing her steps.

Obliged to dart into a tobacconist shop to avoid a face-to-face meeting with the irate lady, Joel waited until she had passed him by, then he came back outside and went to the door Mrs. Farrington had exited only moments before. Affixed to the lintel above the entrance was a sign painted in block letters advertising the office as that of one Thom Newton. Not bothering to knock, Joel pushed open the door and entered the single room.

The arrangement of the furniture was more functional than pleasing, with two scarred desks shoved flush against one another to conserve space. The one concession to possible visitors was a lone ladder-back chair that stood in the far corner, but Joel did not give it a second glance.

"Mr. Newton?" he said to the sour-faced young man who sat behind the smaller desk.

"Not likely," the young man replied, his tone surly. "I'm Burt. Thom's me uncle. But 'e ain't 'ere. You got business wif 'im, you'll 'ave to come back later."

"How much later?"

"A day. Two. Maybe more. 'E don't tell me nofing."

Joel controlled his irritation in the face of the young man's rudeness, but only just. "What is your uncle's occupation?"

"Finds lost persons, 'e does. Mostly blokes as don't wish to be found. You got somebody as needs finding?"

"Not at the moment. I would like some information, however. It regards the veiled lady who was just here."

"The ace of spades?"

"Yes, the widow."

Burt leaned back in his chair, placing his feet on the desk and his hands behind his head, his manner insolent. "Well, maybe I know summit about 'er, and maybe I don't. Me memory ain't what it used to be, but if a bloke was to make it worf me while, could be I'd recall a bit."

From the small pocket in his waistcoat Joel pulled out a coin. Not bothering to look at its value, he tossed the coin onto the desk where it spun on end several times before coming to rest beside Burt's grimy shoes.

At the sight of the gold guinea, Burt sat up straight, his eyes wide with surprise. "She's looking for a bloke," he said. "A soldier. Leastways 'e was a soldier some years ago. The lady wrote to me uncle some time back, the letter come from Maidstone. Me uncle found out summit about the fellow, right enough, but I don't know what. 'E keeps his information in his *nous* box, does Thom Newton. Don't write none of it down for prying eyes to glim."

"And the soldier's name?"

The young man snatched up the gold coin and shoved it deep inside the pocket of his breeches, lest Joel attempt to take it back. "Farrington was the bloke's name. Same as 'ers."

Farrington. Same as 'ers.

Joel pondered Burt's words. All the way back to the inn he tried to work out the relationship existing between the lady to whom he had sent roses and the man she sought.

Was he her brother? An uncle? A cousin?

Oddly enough, Joel favored any one of those possibilities over the less palatable probability that the man was her husband. And yet, the existence of a husband, even one who might not wish to be found, explained the lady's reticence to answer Joel's question regarding the length of her widowed state.

She had been evasive in her reply. Cleverly so, but evasive nonetheless.

Deciding he would have an answer to all his questions— and have it today!—Joel hurried his pace until he very nearly caught up with the veiled figure. Not wanting to confront her in public, however, he paused long enough to allow her to enter the inn, then he followed at a more leisurely pace, being careful not to attract the attention of the manager or one of the porters as he made his way up the staircase.

Joel had no trouble distinguishing her suite from the others, for the lady slammed the door much as she had done the one to Thom Newton's office. Unfortunately for her, the suite door was not so forgiving of her anger; the latch refused to catch and the door swung open an inch or two.

Justifying his actions as necessary for the protection of his cousin, Joel stepped close enough to see inside the room. Mrs. Farrington stood near a loo table, her back to him, and she was conversing with someone he could not see.

"Drat the man!" she said. "He still has not returned."

"How vexing."

The speaker was a young female, but Joel did not think the voice belonged to Miss Mitchell. "So you discovered nothing?"

"Not so," Mrs. Farrington said. "I discovered that I have little tolerance for people who are out of town when I wish to meet with them. And I have even less tolerance for surly young men who care nothing for the concerns of others."

Suddenly she snatched off the heavy veil and tossed it onto the loo table. Though Joel had thought he was ready for any revelations, he was taken aback by the thick chignon fastened at the nape of the lady's smooth neck, the locks not gray as one might expect of a widow, but black and glossy as the backs of the gulls he had watched the day before. And like those birds that seemed to float upon the air above the waters of the channel, Mrs. Farrington moved with an effortless grace, her head held proudly.

As she turned to reply to something the young person had said, Joel got his first look at the lady's face. Here was another revelation, for she was lovely.

She was five or six years older than Miss Mitchell, and not so breathtakingly beautiful as her cousin, yet there was some indefinable quality in her countenance—a quality that would render her handsome long after Miss Mitchell's blond looks had faded.

It was more than the beauty of the lady's eyes—eyes a soft green with flecks of brown, like the leaves of the spotted orchids that grew near the brook at Harcourt Hall—and it was more than her glossy chignon and soft, ivory skin. There was about her a look of character—strength softened by compassion—that transcended a handsome profile and a graceful brow.

"You are the most tolerant person I know," said the unseen young lady, "so do not try to bamboozle me into believing that some surly clerk has cut up your peace."

"Truly, I—"

"What is it? Has it to do with your disappointment at not finding Colonel Farrington, or are you worried about the money giving out before you achieve your goal? And please, be forthright with me, you do me no favor by concealing the truth."

"It is a bit of both, I daresay. However, if we are careful with our expenditures, our funds are sufficient to sustain us through our planned month without—"

"A moment, Gina. The door is ajar. Let me close it so that we may . . ."

Joel stepped away just before a chit not yet out of the

schoolroom came to shut the door, putting an end to his eavesdropping.

So, they had money worries. It was a common enough complaint, and one that afflicted people at all levels of society. Unfortunately, those sufferers sometime chose to employ desperate measures to remedy the situation.

The potentiality that Mrs. Farrington might choose such a remedy, coupled with the proof of Joel's own eyes that the woman was neither who nor what she presented herself to be, should have given him ample to contemplate while he strolled along the busy street. Oddly enough, neither circumstance occupied his thoughts. Foremost in his mind was a thick knot of ebony hair and a pair of brown-flecked green eyes.

"Gina," he repeated softly. "Regina, perhaps? A regal name for a charlatan. But," he added, recalling the proud carriage of her head, "it suits her."

Later that afternoon, as the porter at the Old Ship held the door open for Lord Harcourt to enter the inn, his destination his own suite of rooms, Joel was obliged to step aside to avoid colliding with a tall gentleman who was exiting the building. Noting only that the stranger was dressed in the blue tunic of the light cavalry, Joel bowed slightly. "Your pardon, Lieutenant."

"Not at all, sir, I . . ." The military gentleman paused, apparently surprised when he looked into Joel's face. "Harcourt?"

"Yes?" He gave the younger man his full attention. "Forgive me, Lieutenant. Have we met? I do not seem to recall—"

"Wesley Seaforth," he said, a smile lighting his clear

blue eyes. "Harrow. You were in the fourth form with my older brother, Andrew. I was a first-form boy at the time, so I cannot expect you to have noticed me, especially not when my own brother gave me the cut direct more often than not."

Joel studied the other man's dark blond hair and handsome, almost classical face, trying to subtract the years to fit his vague recollection of his classmate, Andrew Seaforth. The task was not easy, for the schoolboy Joel remembered—a pleasant, if indolent chap—was more inclined to visit the kitchens than the playing fields; while it was obvious from the way Lieutenant Wesley Seaforth's uniform fit his lean physique that *he* preferred sport to food. Still, there was a definite family resemblance.

"How is Andrew?" Joel asked, extending his hand in greeting.

"Corpulent," the lieutenant replied with the irreverence of a younger sibling. Taking Joel's extended hand, he said, "Andrew has too great a fondness for sweet cakes and port wine. Not unlike a certain *royal* older brother."

Joel could not help but respond to the younger man's infectious smile. "A forgivable vice, surely, in a brother or a prince."

"Certainly, sir. Both affable fellows. None better. As a matter of fact, I owe my present address here at the Old Ship to Andrew's largesse, for a Cornet's pay does not normally extend to such luxurious accommodations. Left to my own devices, I should be spending my holiday holed up in far less elegant quarters."

Obliged to step aside to allow an elderly gentleman and his lady access to the inn's entrance, Joel asked the lieutenant if he might offer him refreshments in the coffee room.

"Thank you, but I was on my way to the library to procure

a book for my sister-in-law. It is her birthday next week, and since she is the best of sisters, I would not wish to forget the occasion, which I am likely to do if I do not strike while the iron is hot.''

"I understand. Another time, then.''

"Would you be so kind as to join me, sir?''

Happy for the opportunity of further exercise, Joel readily agreed, and within a matter of minutes the two gentlemen were walking toward the Marine Parade, their long strides taking them to the Royal Marine Library in short time.

It was no surprise that the library was filled to overflowing with smartly dressed ladies and gentlemen, for other than being a place to buy or borrow books, it was a popular gathering place for those of society wishing to see and be seen.

Not a large building by any means, every available bit of wall space was filled with floor to ceiling shelves, upon which were stacked books to tempt every taste. Alongside the novels of Maria Edgeworth and Walter Scott, and whichever writer was currently in vogue, were books of poetry as well as tomes for the edification of the mind. On special display were guidebooks lauding the beauty of Brighton and the many benefits of sea bathing upon the health of both the robust and the infirm.

While a few of the library's patrons walked about scanning the shelves for likely purchases, others occupied the wooden benches or made use of the long refectory tables to peruse books or current periodicals. Still others did not even feign an interest in the books; these were mostly groups of gentlemen who stood about conversing, their attention never fully divorced from the entrance lest they miss an opportunity to ogle one of the young ladies who came and went with regularity.

Joel chose to traverse the length of the shelves with his new acquaintance while that gentleman searched out a book for his sister-in-law's birthday, but no less than the other gentlemen did he ignore the opening of the entrance door and the appearance of a young woman accompanied by a veiled chaperone. However, he doubted the group of oglers spared a moment's attention for the woman who most piqued his interest.

"By George!" Lieutenant Seaforth uttered, after noticing the direction of Joel's gaze. "Who is that vision in the primrose bonnet?"

Joel tore his attention from the veiled figure and glanced at the young lady who had so bewitched his cousin.

"Miss Constance Mitchell," he said.

The lieutenant spared a moment from staring at the lady in yellow to look at Joel. "You are acquainted with her?"

"Slightly."

"Enough for an introduction?"

Since Joel had already formed the intention of approaching the two women, he readily agreed to presenting his new acquaintance. Seaforth was both personable and well favored, and his presence should enliven the meeting. And though there were no guarantees, the introduction of a handsome gentleman in uniform might even divert the focus of the younger lady's ambition away from Mr. Oliver Drayson.

"I will be happy to introduce you," he said.

The young man clapped him on the shoulder. "By George, Harcourt, this must be my lucky day! First I chance to meet you, then I have the honor of an introduction to the most beautiful girl I have ever beheld."

Books and sisters-in-law were all but forgotten as the two gentlemen crossed the room to make their bows before the ladies.

"Mrs. Farrington," Joel said. "Well met, ma'am."

"Lord Harcourt," Regina replied rather breathlessly. For the first time since she had donned the detested veil, she was glad of its presence. Otherwise, every person in the room would have known by the warmth in her face just how unsettling she found this encounter with the gentleman who had sent her roses.

"May I present Lieutenant Wesley Seaforth?" Lord Harcourt asked. "His brother and I were at school together."

Regina felt on safer ground now that there were formalities that had to be gotten through, so she inclined her head, granting permission for the introduction.

"An honor, ma'am," the lieutenant said, bowing over her hand.

"Lieutenant Seaforth, allow me to make you known to my cousin, Miss Constance Mitchell."

As if spellbound, he gazed at the young lady in primrose. "Miss Mitchell," he said, the tone of his voice reverent as he spoke her name.

"A . . . a pleasure, sir," she replied.

The lieutenant shook his head slowly. "I assure you, fair lady, the pleasure is entirely mine."

Since the arrival of the three cousins in Brighton, dozens of men had wangled introductions to Constance, but until that moment, Regina had never seen anything more than polite interest upon her cousin's face. However, the situation was much different when Lieutenant Seaforth made his bow. While the military gentleman said all that was proper, Constance blushed prettily, paying close attention to his every word.

Regina smiled, not at all surprised by Constance's reaction, for here was a gentlemen even Felicity must approve. Though a second son, Lieutenant Seaforth was apparently well connected, and if his easy, pleasant manners were not enough to engage the interest of any young lady, there was always his appearance. He was as handsome as he could stare. A blond, Nordic god.

And he was not nearly so *old* as Lord Harcourt!

Another smile pulled at Regina's mouth as she wondered what his lordship would say if he should discover Felicity's opinion of his vast accumulation of years.

"Madam," said that *elderly* gentleman, bringing Regina's thoughts back to the present, "I was just asking your cousin if she could recommend a book for Lieutenant Seaforth's sister-in-law. I undertook to assist him in his search," he added, "but I fear I was of little help. Perhaps Miss Mitchell may succeed where I have failed."

"I shall be happy to try," Constance replied quietly.

"Mrs. Farrington?" Seaforth asked very properly.

Regina readily excused the couple. Not for the world would she have detained her cousin, for though the young lady's lovely countenance was as serene as ever, those who knew Constance could read her true feelings by the telling light in her eyes—a light that made those dark blue orbs sparkle like gems. For her part, Regina was delighted that Constance had met someone who could elicit such a response.

So, too, was the young lady delighted. If the truth be known, Constance's heart was beating so rapidly she wondered how she managed to walk the short distance from the door to the shelf where the books she preferred were displayed. Never had she seen such a handsome man. No, not handsome, *beautiful*.

Lieutenant Seaforth was everything she had ever dreamed of in a man: tall, slender yet muscular, and with the blond hair and blue eyes of a Norse god. As well, he possessed a ready smile and an easy manner that must make any lady comfortable in his presence. From the first, Constance found herself able to speak freely with him, almost as if they were friends of long standing.

"Are you enjoying your stay in Brighton, Lieutenant?"

His smile went directly to her heart. "I am now, Miss Mitchell."

In the past fortnight, Constance had been flattered and complimented by some of society's most accomplished flirts, but those practiced phrases had left her feeling nothing but embarrassment. It was odd, then, that the lieutenant's simple declaration had pleased her out of all proportion.

"And you?" he asked, looking at her as if her answer was important to him. "Are you happy that you came to Brighton?"

"Yes," she said quietly. "I am now."

Though Regina had been absorbed for several moments in watching the handsome pair approach the stacks, she chanced to return her attention to Lord Harcourt in time to catch a rather smug expression upon his face. If she had not seen that look, Regina might have been tempted to believe him no more than the genial mediator he had appeared. However, she had seen it, and as a result she realized the man had purposefully thrown the lieutenant and Constance together.

His lordship's design Regina could only imagine, but two possibilities occurred to her. The first, that he wanted to divert Constance's attention away from his cousin Oliver, and the second, that he wished to procure a few moments private conversation with the young lady's chaperone.

The first conjecture seemed most probable, yet it was the second that accelerated the pace of Regina's heart.

Foolish, foolish female!

Choosing not to dwell overlong on a supposition whose reality most likely existed only in her own mind, she said, "This meeting is most propitious, sir, for I have been wanting to speak with you."

Lord Harcourt lifted one rather satirical eyebrow. "I am intrigued, madam. What is it you wished to speak to me about?"

"The roses, my lord. They did, indeed, smell sweet."

"They met with your approval, then?"

"I should be hard to please if they had not. I believe I may safely say they are the most beautiful flowers I have ever received."

He leaned rather close to her, and since she stood almost flush with the wall and had no place to retreat, she was obliged to endure his proximity with what calmness she could summon. When he spoke, his voice was hushed, almost a whisper. "There are those who feel the rose is too secretive a flower."

Regina felt prickles of sensation run up the back of her neck, though whether the cause stemmed from his lordship's closeness or his choice of words, she could not say. "Secretive?"

"According to the florist, the rose hides its true beauty behind a protective covering."

"It . . . it does?"

"Without a doubt," he replied, stressing the final word. "And the fellow informed me that if I wished to see the *real* flower, I must carefully remove the outer petals that shield it."

Regina felt those prickles again.

Slowly, deliberately Lord Harcourt touched the tip of his forefinger to one of the folds of her veil, then he traced the silken crease from somewhere near her temple to just above her madly beating heart. "Perhaps," he said quietly, "it is you who should remove that protective covering."

Regina licked suddenly dry lips. "Sir, you—"

"After all," he interrupted, "the roses are in your possession."

Regina's knees threatened to give way beneath her.

He knows. Somehow or other, he knows I am not what I pretend to be.

Chapter Four

He knows!

During the entire trip back to The Knight's Arms, Regina could think of nothing else but Lord Harcourt's thinly veiled threat. Somehow he had guessed that she was enacting a charade. But how? What could have betrayed her? And what was more important, now that he knew, what if *he* betrayed her?

He could do nothing to hurt her, of course, but such a revelation, if it became the latest *en dit* in this small village, could ruin her cousin's chances of making an eligible connection. Neither Felicity nor Constance possessed the skills needed to earn their livings, and they depended upon the successful outcome of this sojourn to insure their futures.

He will not expose them! Not if I have anything to say in the matter.

"Drat the man!"

"Who?" Constance asked. "You do not refer to Lieutenant Seaforth? Oh, tell me you do not."

They were within earshot of the entrance to the inn, so Regina hushed her. "We cannot speak of it now. We will be overheard."

Ordinarily a most biddable girl, Constance would not be put off. "You liked him, surely? Of course you did," she continued, "for who could not? He is everything that is amiable. And so handsome. And kind. Not a bit intimidating, as are so many of the gentlemen we have met."

The anxiety in Constance's voice finally penetrated Regina's own anxiety, and she turned to look into her cousin's face. Tears glistened in her eyes.

"My dear," Regina said, taking the young lady's hand and squeezing it reassuringly, "forgive me for distressing you. Whatever my present concern, you may rest assured it has nothing to do with Lieutenant Seaforth. As you say, *that* gentleman is everything that is amiable."

Constance sighed. "Then who has—?"

"Please. Ask me no questions at this time, for I need to think. Once I have had an opportunity to know my own feelings, we shall discuss the matter in detail."

Obliged to respect Regina's wishes, Constance said no more upon the subject until she and Felicity were alone in their shared bedchamber that evening. "I cannot think what put Gina so out of countenance this afternoon."

"She said nothing more?" Felicity asked.

"No more than I have related."

Felicity removed a plain lawn night rail from beneath her bed pillow then went behind the dressing screen and began to disrobe. One item at a time flew through the air as she tossed her schoolgirl disguise onto a much abused rout chair that stood beside the washstand. Only after she untied the swath of material that bound her bosom did she speak.

"One would think a female with no more womanly attributes than I possess would have no need to bind herself in this most uncomfortable manner. I cannot credit that I am obliged to take such steps to conceal that which under normal circumstances is barely noticeable."

Because this was not a new complaint regarding her disguise, the young lady was not surprised to receive no sympathy from her older sister. She did, however, peer around the screen to see if Constance was listening. She was not attending; not if the moonstruck look upon her face was anything by which to judge.

"Have you heard a word I said?"

"What?" Constance said, bestirring herself enough to gaze in her sister's direction.

"Jupiter and Mars! Never tell me you are still thinking about that Lieutenant Seashore."

"Seaforth," Constance corrected, the word a mere whisper. "Lieutenant Wesley Seaforth. Is it not a lovely name?"

Actually, Felicity thought the appellation sounded rather ridiculous, but she kept her opinion to herself. They were come to Brighton to find her sister a husband, and so far this was the first gentleman in whom Constance had shown any sort of interest. Though how that could be when she had almost daily proof of Mr. Oliver Drayson's devotion, Felicity could not understand.

"Could it be anything to do with your lieutenant that sent Gina to her bedchamber directly when you returned from the Library?"

Constance blushed hotly. "He is not *my* lieutenant."

"*The* lieutenant, then. Did Gina take him in dislike?"

"She said not. And I believe her, for she was most cordial to Seaforth when Lord Harcourt made him known to us."

"Lord Harcourt? The gentleman who sent you the roses?"

"Yes. It was he who suggested I might help Seaforth find a book suitable for his sister-in-law's birthday. While Seaforth and I searched the shelves, Lord Harcourt was so kind as to keep Gina company."

After pulling the night rail down over her head, Felicity left the dressing screen and made a running leap onto the bed. Once she made herself comfortable, with her legs hugged to her chest and her chin resting upon one knee, she studied her sister. "Do you know what syntax and semantics are?"

"What a foolish question. Of course I do."

"Then I suppose you know why Lord Harcourt wrote those words on the card that came with the roses he sent?"

Constance shrugged her shoulders dismissively. "I cannot think why anyone would write such a thing. As for Lord Harcourt, I have exchanged fewer than a dozen words with the man, so I know little of his character or his humors. Whatever his motives for such an illogical note, I cannot explain them."

Could their cousin explain them? Something told Felicity it was a distinct possibility. And if Gina understood the note, it was conceivable that the roses were meant for her and not Constance. But if they were, why had Gina said nothing?

The question kept the young lady awake for fully ten minutes, but on the morrow her thoughts returned to her cousin and Lord Harcourt. After much consideration, Felicity decided that it was *she* who had assumed the flowers were for her sister. So focused was she on her campaign to see Constance married before the month was out that she automatically numbered any gentleman among her sister's admirers without even considering another likelihood. It simply had not occurred to her that any man would look elsewhere when Constance was before him.

"Jupiter and Mars! What presumption on my part. And it was grossly unfair to Gina."

Their cousin was a wonderful person and still quite beautiful despite her six and twenty years; furthermore, it was conceivable that a man of thirty might consider six and twenty young. Her age notwithstanding, Gina was deserving of future happiness, and if there was even the remotest chance that she had become an object of admiration to Lord Harcourt, then Felicity was ready to do all within her power to see the gentleman had the opportunity to better his aquaintance.

She had not long to wait to put her plan into action, for shortly after the ladies had broken their fast, a note arrived from his lordship, addressed to Mrs. Farrington. After giving the missive a quick perusal, Gina handed it to Felicity, instructing her to read it aloud.

"My dear madam," she read, "Lieutenant Seaforth and I extend an invitation to you and both your cousins to join us for a drive to Cuthbert House, near Lewes, for an al fresco nuncheon in the gardens there. The day promises to be balmy, so do say you will come. Unless I receive instructions to the contrary, we will fetch you and the misses Mitchell some time around eleven."

"Famous!" Constance said, her eyes no less bright than the sunshine that peeked through the curtains at the windows, spilling warm light upon the carpeted floor. "How I should enjoy a picnic."

"You two go," Gina said, lifting the *Times* so that it

obscured her face. "I have no wish to ride about the countryside."

"No!" Felicity said.

At her vehemence, Constance and Gina both stared. "What I mean is, surely a chaperone is wanted to satisfy the proprieties."

Her cousin took refuge behind the newspaper once agin, but not before Felicity had time to note the pink that stained her cheeks.

"If you are concerned about the propriety of such an excursion," Gina responded, "you may take Bessie along. No doubt she would enjoy the outing, for she has had scarcely more occasion than you to partake of the delights of Brighton and its environs."

Felicity felt like giving her cousin a good shake. *Why must she make this more difficult than need be?*

Thinking fast, Felicity said, "I shall need Bessie to remain here with me."

Gina put the paper down at last. "Remain with you? But surely you would not miss this opportunity to get out? If memory serves, scarce two days ago you were complaining about being obliged to remain in the suite. Now, here is an acceptable outing—one in which a schoolroom miss might well participate—and you speak of staying behind."

"I . . . I have the headache this morning, and I believe I should feel better for a lie down with a cold compress upon my brow."

Immediately Constance was all solicitousness. "Dearest, are you sickening from something?" She looked across the table at their cousin, concern wrinkling her brow. "Felicity is never ill. And if she has ever had the headache, I never knew of it. Should we send for a doctor, do you think?"

"No, no!" Felicity said. " 'Tis but a trifling throb. Nothing for either of you to be concerned about. Depend upon it, after an hour or two in a darkened room, I shall be right as a trivet. And I beg of you, do not think of refusing Lord Harcourt's invitation on my account, for I shall do much better for a little solitude."

Felicity stood her ground, and aided by her sister's confession that she had long fostered a desire to see the gardens at Cuthbert House, she finally persuaded Gina to relent and act as Constance's chaperone.

"Kindest of cousins," Constance said. Pleased to have all settled, she gave Gina a hug then rushed to her bedchamber to search out an ensemble suitable for a drive across the downs.

The gentlemen arrived just as the lacquered case clock that stood at the bend of the staircase in the corridor chimed the hour of eleven. Felicity, postponing those recuperative two hours in the darkened room, sat at the loo table, her chair facing the door so that she might have a clear view of both gentlemen while also observing the reactions of her relatives.

When Bessie opened the door, Lieutenant Seaforth entered first, carrying a nosegay of delicate pink rosebuds secured in a silver filigree holder. It needed only one glance at that handsome gentleman for Felicity to understand why her sister's cheeks rivaled the flowers. Tall and slender, with dark blond hair and blue eyes, he was a masculine version of Constance.

"Mrs. Farrington," he said, crossing the room to make his bow before Gina, "I thank you for agreeing to this outing."

"You are welcome, Lieutenant."

The conventions satisfied, he turned to Constance, upon his face a look of adoration only just held in check. "Miss Mitchell," he said, offering her the nosegay.

The gentleman who followed Seaforth into the room could be none other than Lord Harcourt, and though his corbeau coat and cream waistcoat could not compare with the lieutenant's smart blue tunic, there was about the man an air of authority that would render him noticeable in a parade ground filled with cavalry officers.

He was even taller than Seaforth, with a more muscular build, and Felicity could find nothing to dislike in his dark brown hair or his brown eyes—eyes that seemed to smile at her now as though he and she shared a secret.

"You must be Miss Felicity," he said, making her a very courtly bow. "I have been looking forward to this meeting."

"You have, sir? Why is that?"

"I was curious," he said, "to discover how much younger you were than Miss Mitchell."

Though she heard a strangled gasp come from beneath Gina's thick veil, Felicity tried to remain calm. There was no reason to assume any hidden meaning behind his lordship's remark. After all, no one else had seen through her disguise. Why should she suspect Lord Harcourt of having done so?

"Sir," she said, attempting to put a brave face on it, "surely you are too much the gentleman to ask a lady to reveal her age."

He spared a glance at Gina before returning his attention to her. "Naturally I would not be so rag-mannered as to ask such a question of Mrs. Farrington. Nor would I ask it of a lady of . . . oh, let us say seventeen or eighteen years.

However, I cannot think, Miss Felicity, that you would consider it an impertinence. After all, what can a chit of your tender years have to hide?''

"Lord Harcourt!" Gina said, choosing that moment to hurry across the room, her hand outstretched in greeting. "Can there be any among us who has not hidden away in his or her heart at least one thought or action?"

"First semantics, and now conundrums," Lord Harcourt replied. "Madam, you are a woman of many parts." Having said this, he took her proffered hand and lifted the fingers all the way to his lips.

The instant his lips touched her skin, Gina snatched her hand away. "Sir," she said, her voice not quite steady, "since I am persuaded you will not wish to leave your horses standing overlong, perhaps we should be on our way."

"Capital idea," Seaforth said, offering his right arm to Constance. When she had placed her hand in the crook of his elbow, he turned and offered his left arm to Felicity. "Miss Felicity, may I have the pleasure?"

"Thank you. Lieutenant, but I shall not be joining you. I have the headache."

Seaforth said all that was proper, wishing her a speedy recovery, but Lord Harcourt gave her a look that said he was not deceived. "A pity," he said. "Another time, perhaps."

"Perhaps," she replied noncommittally.

Once the foursome had quit the room, Felicity expelled her breath noisily, relieved to be free of Lord Harcourt's much-too-discerning scrutiny. "Another time?" she repeated. "Not if I have any say in the matter."

* * *

Regina had assumed they would all travel together, but she was disabused of that notion the instant she exited The Knight's Arms. To her dismay, standing just outside the entrance to the inn was not the staid coach she expected—a landau or a berlin, one that would accommodate the entire party—but two equipages. One of the vehicles was his lordship's own curricle, pulled by a pair of handsome bays; the other was a hired whiskey, between the shafts a fresh and spirited roan.

While one of the inn grooms stood at the roan's head to hold it in check, a liveried postilion held the reins of the bays as well as those of an impressive chestnut gelding with snow white stockings.

Regina stared at the gelding. One of the gentlemen meant to ride. She hoped it was Lord Harcourt, but on the chance that it was not, she mentally arranged the seating so that she and Constance occupied the same carriage. In that way, she need have as little contact as possible with his lordship.

Unfortunately, Lieutenant Seaforth spoiled her neat arrangements by blithely assisting Constance into the whiskey then springing up beside her. After taking the reins and tossing a coin to the groom, he tipped his hat to Regina and let the straining horse have its way. While Regina stood helplessly, watching the roan as it clip-clopped briskly down the cobbled street, Lord Harcourt grasped her by the elbow and helped her to climb aboard his fashionable two-wheeler.

Please let him ride!

"Take the gelding back to the stable," he instructed the postilion.

As Regina silently cursed the fates, Lord Harcourt sprang up beside her, seated himself, and took the reins.

"The fellow was prepared to ride one of the bays while you and Miss Felicity occupied the curricle," he explained. "However, since our plans have changed, and we are shy one lady, I need not ride alone, but may give myself the pleasure of your company for the entire journey."

Pleasure was the last thing Regina anticipated. The prospect of being alone with Lord Harcourt, and in such close proximity, filled her with nothing but dread.

During the next few minutes, as they traversed the Steine, then bore right toward the Lewes Road, the jingle of the horses' bridles and the click of carriage wheels were drummed out by the pounding of the pulse in Regina's temples. That pulse beat even louder when they reached the open road, and Lord Harcourt was no longer obliged to give his full attention to his driving. To Regina's horror, when he sat back, his broad shoulders filled the space, forcing her to hug the sides of the curricle to avoid feeling the constant bunching and relaxing of the muscles in his arm.

Though she was certain he was aware of her plight, he made no effort to shift his own position in order to give her more room. Instead, he remarked rather blandly, "You are quite comfortable, I trust."

Regina fought an urge to shove him from the moving carriage. She might even have acted upon that desire if he had not chosen that moment to give the horses the office to quicken their pace. The bays began to gallop along at a smart clip, and the resulting breeze that whipped past Regina toyed mercilessly with the folds of her veil, threatening to lift it, bonnet and all, from her head. As a result, she was obliged to hold to the sides of the seat with one hand while trying to contain her flying veil with the other.

"I have a suggestion," Lord Harcourt said, amusement in his voice. "You could dispense with the trappings of your status. There is no one to see you but me."

The wind was not the only thing toying with her: his lordship was enjoying himself immensely.

"I have a suggestion, too, my lord. But I doubt you would grant my wish."

He laughed aloud. "Madam, can it be that you wish me bodily harm? Ought I to be frightened?"

When she did not reply, he said, "But perhaps I misunderstand. Who can know what is in a speaker's heart when one is not allowed to see that person's eyes. *Windows to the soul,* I believe they are called. And rightly so, for by looking into the eyes, it is often possible to discern those unspoken truths."

He slowed the horses to a canter, then to a trot so that the veil no longer blew all about, but Regina did not relax. Nor was she lulled into a false sense of security by the warmth of the sun or the beauty of the road that undulated gently through the hills and valleys. Instead she waited, her body a mass of taut nerves, for Lord Harcourt had not finished tormenting her, and she knew it.

"There are those," he said, "who believe that blue eyes give up their secrets more readily, but I do not agree. In my experience, the most revealing eyes are green. Especially green with flecks of golden brown."

Regina caught her breath. How did he know the color of her eyes?

"I am persuaded you know the color I describe."

"I . . . I am certain I do not, sir."

He gave her a sidelong look. "But you must have seen

such eyes a million times. Like those of an Irish colleen, they are most often framed by hair the color of polished ebony. Thick, shiny tresses drawn away from the face into a modest chignon. No fringe to mar the symmetry of the forehead, no distracting curls dangling before the ears. Just a simple—''

''Sir! I will not be taunted in this way. If you have something to say, then say it and have done.''

''But I thought I had already said it. As for taunting you, I must protest. I have done naught, madam, but invite you to dispense with your very cumbersome veil so that you might enjoy this balmy weather.''

Weary of the entire charade, Regina reached up with both hands and lifted the black silk. She could not even guess how this man she had known but a few days had managed to describe her appearance so accurately, but in view of his knowledge, there seemed little point in clinging to her disguise.

''I wish you joy of your victory, sir.'' Folding the veil back over her head, she let it fall where it would about her shoulders. ''My capitulation is now complete.''

While she clasped her hands in her lap and stared straight ahead, Joel studied her angry profile. He could not look away. The late morning sun gave her ivory skin the shimmer of fine pearls, but it was not her complexion that held him. Nor was it the resolute chin, the small, straight nose, or the soft, sculpted cheek. It was her mouth that captured his attention. Though she frowned at the moment, nothing could detract from that lovely mouth, or from the full, satiny, kissable lips.

Kissable? Damn the woman! And damn his own foolishness for all but forcing her to remove that veil.

''Odd,'' he said, less to break the silence than to give

his thoughts something other than her lips to ponder, "that one female should endeavor to add years to her age while the other attempts to reduce the number. Would you care to explain to me the reasoning behind such a plan?"

Though she did not look at him, he heard the quick intake of her breath, saw the slight flaring of her nostrils. "The actions of my family—odd though they may appear to you—cannot concern you in any way."

"Ah, but there you are wrong, my lovely colleen."

"Do not call me that!"

"Do not call you what? Mine? Lovely? Colleen?"

"You know my name. If you must speak to me, address me properly."

"Very well, Regina."

She turned to him then, and her eyes were afire with indignation. "You have now passed the bounds of what is pleasing, Lord Harcourt. I gave you no leave to use my given name."

"True. But I find I do not care for *Mrs. Farrington*. And since you do not approve my other choices, that leaves me with no other option. Regina. I like it, by the way."

"Sir, you are no gentleman."

"And you, madam, are no widow."

Those green eyes grew wide with surprise. "Do not be absurd, sir. Of course I am a widow."

"I doubt that Mr. Thom Newton would agree."

Her face lost its color. "Who?"

"Mr. Thom Newton."

She swallowed with difficulty. "I do not believe I know the person."

"No? Pray, allow me to jog your memory. The corner

of North Street. Stuffy little office. Surely you remember his nephew, Burt? Insolent fellow. Sour-faced. With dirty shoes.''

Joel could see she was trying to think of some story that would convince him she had no knowledge of Thom Newton or his nephew. That she was having no success was obvious from the trapped-animal look in her eyes. No wonder she had chosen to don a veil, the lady had no talent for lying.

''Well?'' he drawled.

As if suddenly remembering that the best defense was a good offense, Regina said, ''How dare you follow me as though I were some common criminal.''

''Madam,'' he said, ''the word *common* never entered my mind.''

She gasped as though she had been struck. ''Stop the carriage! I will not spend one more minute in your company.''

When he did not slow the horses, she sat forward, as if preparing to alight whether or not he heeded her order to stop.

''Do not be ridiculous, Regina. We have covered at least five miles since leaving Brighton, and it is three more miles before we reach Cuthbert House.''

''Three miles are nothing to me,'' she said, her words clipped. ''I have lived my entire life in the country, and I am accustomed to long walks.''

''Be that as it may, *I* am not accustomed to setting unattended females down in the middle of the road. You may not think me a gentleman, but I have not sunk to such a level as that.''

Her face determined, Regina lifted the hem of her skirt

above her boot tops, then she scooted to the edge of the seat.

Though Joel was not convinced she would jump, he was afraid to risk the possibility. "Do not!" he commanded, catching her wrist in a firm grasp.

Chapter Five

Regina did not struggle to break free of his grasp, instead she stared at his hand upon her wrist, her expression cold enough to cause frost in July. "I do not like to be constrained."

"Then sit back!" Joel said. In a calmer tone he added, "Please. I will stop the curricle, but you must allow me to find a suitable spot to pull over, in the event that another vehicle should wish to pass."

The instant she complied with his request to sit back, he let go of her wrist. Neither of them spoke for the next three or four minutes, until they encountered a narrow country lane. It was little more than a cart path, and ordinarily Joel would not have subjected his horses to such rough ground; but he had given Regina his word, and he would not renege.

After they turned onto the lane, he held the bays in

check, keeping them to a walk until they came to a little copse of yew trees, where he pulled them to a stop.

"And now," he said, turning to Regina, "we need to talk."

She did not make it easy, sitting primly with her hands in her lap and her gaze fixed upon a whitebeam tree whose shimmering leaves fluttered in the breeze—staring ahead as though to look at him would have been a betrayal of her code of ethics. "Talk?" she repeated. "I am of the opinion that enough has been said already. Too much, actually."

"For which I offer you my humblest apologies. 'Twas but a jest, Regina, albeit a jest in poor taste, for I do not believe you to be a criminal."

When she remained silent, her attention still fixed upon the silvery leaves of the whitebeam tree, he continued. "Try if you can see this from my viewpoint. I discover, quite by accident, that you are not the middle-aged person you present yourself to be. Then, when I meet your cousin, a young lady fully grown, she has assumed the guise of a schoolroom miss. You must admit, Regina, that such circumstances give rise to all manner of unfavorable speculation."

She admitted nothing.

"Naturally," he said, "I was curious—as I am persuaded that anyone would be—why the two of you should choose to play such parts. I merely offered you an opportunity to explain your actions and those of your cousin."

"I owe you no explanations!" she said, turning upon him a look even colder than before. "You have done nothing to earn my confidences, and it is the greatest impertinence for you to attempt to force that which I do not wish to give."

Once begun, she seemed bent upon continuing. "You are little more than a stranger to me, Lord Harcourt. Until a few days ago, I did not even know of your existence, and this being true, I cannot understand why you have taken it upon yourself to become concerned in my affairs. If by some convoluted reasoning you have concluded that I would welcome such intrusions, then you have widely mistaken my character."

The coldness in her voice, a startling contrast to the angry fire in her eyes, convinced Joel that he must do something immediately to reassure her that he did not wish to force confidences from her. Otherwise, she was quite capable of refusing to receive him in the future, thereby making it impossible for him to look out for the interests of his cousin.

Joel had promised his Aunt Beatrix to discover what game the three women were playing, and from what he had learned so far, at least two of them were most definitely up to something. What, he did not know. And if Regina gave him his *conge*, he might never know; of a certainty, not until after his cousin had been snared in some feminine trap.

Damn! I have been too precipitous.

It was easy to see his error now, of course. He had rushed his fences, acted with less finesse than a green boy, and it behooved him to pick himself up and try whatever necessary to regain the lost ground. For that reason, he decided he must do what he could to reinstate himself in Regina's good graces. He was not without experience where the fair sex were concerned. He knew how to placate a recalcitrant lady. He would flatter her. Charm her, if necessary. Do whatever was needed to win her over.

With those objectives in mind, he gave his full attention

to the bays' reins, not looking up from his contemplation of the ribbons that rested easily within his gloved fingers. "You are right, of course," he said, his voice quiet, "I crossed the line of what is pleasing."

He inhaled deeply, then exhaled slowly. "What is worse, I crossed the line of civility as well. As you observed, we are virtual strangers, and in letting my curiosity run away with me, I have offended you." He turned to look at her then, with what he hoped was a remorseful countenance. "For this, I offer you my apologies, and pray that you will find it in your heart to forgive me."

She was tempted to forgive him; he could see it in her face. It was there in the softening of the corners of her rigidly held lips; it was evident in the lessening of the fire in her green eyes.

"If nothing else," he said, his tone just the right blend of self-deprecation and amusement, "there is now someone before whom you may relax your guard. Since I already know that you are come to Brighton *incognito*, you may brush aside your veil when in my company. You can be yourself without fear of the consequences."

He lowered his voice almost to a whisper. "I hope I need not tell you that you may trust in my discretion. You may ask anyone who knows me, they will confirm that I still retain a *few* gentlemanlike qualities."

Pink stained her cheeks. "Sir, when I said you were not a gentleman, I spoke in anger. I should never have given voice to such a remark."

"Think nothing of it, ma'am. In fact, it would please me if we could totally expunge the last half hour from our memories. If that were possible, perhaps we might start anew."

He removed his right glove and held his hand out to her. "May we begin again?"

After only a moment's hesitation, she placed her hand in his. Her palm was soft against his, the skin smooth and warm, almost *innocent*. Then she looked up at him, and there was a shyness in her eyes—a shyness that caused a momentary pang of guilt inside his chest.

Foolishness, he told himself. Why should he experience feelings of guilt? The woman was a schemer, and he was merely following her example. His actions were no more reprehensible than hers, and at least his motives were unselfish. After all, he was doing this for his cousin.

Despite her earlier reservations, Regina thoroughly enjoyed the last three miles of their journey. Now that the air had been cleared between them, Lord Harcourt proved a delightful traveling companion. One might even say a charming one.

It was as though he had set himself the task of entertaining her. Beguiling the minutes with commentary concerning the pleasures in store for her at the much-celebrated gardens at Cuthbert House, he phrased his comments in such a way that they often brought a smile to her lips.

"The gardens are reputed to be quite beautiful," he said. "By my reckoning, however, their greatest attraction is that they were *not* designed by the great Capability Brown."

She could not help laughing. "Sir, you are a Philistine."

"A distinct possibility, ma'am. But do you never tire of hearing of fireplaces by Adam, and gardens by Brown?"

"And nonsense by Harcourt?"

He chuckled. It was a pleasant sound, deep and spontaneous and uninhibited, giving rise to a similar response in Regina.

"You have a lovely smile," he said softly.

The compliment caught her offguard and made the breath catch in her throat. Was he flirting with her? Could that be possible? Regina was not experienced enough in dalliance to judge accurately, nor could she say whether the notion pleased her or gave her cause for concern.

Unbidden, she recalled the warmth of his touch when he had asked if they might begin their acquaintance anew. She had laid her hand in his, and at the feel of the slightly roughened texture of his palm, she had experienced an almost overpowering desire to move her palm back and forth against his—to explore the hardened skin with her fingertips.

She had managed to quell that totally inappropriate desire, but now, upon hearing his compliment and the sound of the softly spoken words, that longing resurfaced. Embarrassed at the wantonness of her thinking, Regina turned to stare at the beginning of a massive brick wall to her right, afraid she might somehow reveal her thoughts and give Lord Harcourt a disgust of her.

"We are almost there," he said.

Happy to return to more mundane conversation, she asked him how he knew.

"The wall. It shields the thirty-acre deer park from prying eyes. But not, I take leave to remind you, because it was designed by a gentleman other than *you-know-who.*"

If Regina had doubted the truth of his words, she would have been obliged to abandon her disbelief the instant they passed through the low-slung wooden gates—gates that gave access to the long, beech tree-lined drive of Cuthbert House.

To the far left, nestled in gently folded downs, were lush green pasture lands dotted with groups of white sheep, some grazing, others lying on the soft turf, their legs tucked beneath their fluffy bodies, as though they posed for some unseen landscape artist.

In the distance to the right was a large country house, its impressive double-door entrance bordered by carefully pruned hawthorns, their pink-tinged white blossoms so thick they were evident from the road. Faced in the knapped flint of the chalk downs, the main structure was four stories tall while the extensions to either side were three stories, with virtually dozens of chimneys jutting from the roof lines.

Regina could not help her quick intake of breath.

"Impressed?" he asked, one cynical eyebrow raised in question.

"Who would not be," she replied. "One can only wonder how the gardens—whoever their designer—can possibly live up to the splendor of the edifice and the park. The house wants only one single mantelpiece by Adam, and I shall be in a fair way of falling in love with its owner."

Harcourt chuckled. "Sight unseen?"

"Oh, I have seen quite enough, I assure you.

"I meant the owner," he said.

"As did I," she replied.

His lordship was still laughing when he halted the horses near a gravel rectangle roped off on three sides. Within the confines of the ropes were four other carriages, one of them Lieutenant Seaforth's hired whiskey.

"I'll see to your 'orses, Guv," said a wizened, gnome of a fellow who seemed to materialize out of thin air. Of indeterminate age, though possessed of a gray beard that reached almost to his chest, he was dressed in a leather weskit several sizes too big for his thin frame, rough tweed breeches, and a beaver hat badly in need of reblocking.

As he drew near, the little man touched his fingers to his hat brim in a show of respect. "Those be fine bits of blood, Guv, if you'll pardon me saying so. Prime goers, I'll be bound. But never you fear, I know 'ow to look after such cattle, I do."

Without waiting for permission, he caught the leader's halter and led the team toward the rope enclosure. Once there, he tethered the pair by means of a six-foot length of tack, then he scotched the wheel of the curricle with a wedge of wood.

"Everything'll be right and tight now, Guv," he said, holding out a remarkably filthy hand for the expected largesse.

After tossing a shilling to the fellow, who seemed to disappear into that vague place from which he had come, Lord Harcourt hopped down from the carriage, then he turned to assist Regina to alight.

As he put his hands on either side of her waist, then lifted her down with an ease that left her all too aware of his strength, Regina fought to think of something to say. Anything to divert her thoughts from his lordship's powerful hands; anything to still her whirling senses.

"Was he of *this* world?" she asked, looking at that place where the strange little man had stood only moments ago.

Lord Harcourt shook his head. "Who can say?" He had dropped his hands from her waist, but he had not stepped away, and his attention seemed concentrated upon Regina's face.

At his continued closeness, Regina's senses fairly tingled with awareness of his height and breadth.

"Did you not find his appearance amazing?" she muttered.

An ironic smile pulled at the corners of his lordship's well-shaped mouth. "I did not find the little man's appearance nearly so amazing as I fear Seaforth may find yours."

Her wits undermined by that smile, Regina did not immediately take his meaning regarding Seaforth and her appearance.

"Your veil," he whispered, as though the item's existence was a secret they shared.

Suddenly recalling where she was and who she was supposed to be, Regina reached behind her neck to bring the detested covering forward. Unfortunately, with no looking glass to aid her, she found it impossible to separate the layers of material. "Drat this detestable thing!"

For the second time that day, Lord Harcourt caught her by the wrist, only this time he did so with a gentle touch. "Careful," he said, "or you will tear it. Allow me."

Standing so close to her their bodies were mere inches apart, he lowered her arms to her side, then he reached over her shoulders, catching the hem of the heavy silk. With his chin practically touching her forehead, the clean, woodsy fragrance of his shaving soap filled her nostrils, teasing her senses in a way that made her knees decidedly wobbly.

Regina breathed deeply of the masculine scent, wishing she dared lean forward that last little bit, close enough to rest her face against his neck cloth, near enough to feel . . .

"Here we go," he said, shattering her fantasy.

Slowly he raised the veil up and over her head, but before he let it fall to cover her face, he paused. There was a question in his eyes. For just a moment, Regina's heart threatened to leap right out of her chest, for she had the oddest sensation that he had guessed her thoughts.

When his gaze traveled to her mouth and lingered there, she was convinced he meant to kiss her, and she closed her eyes in anticipation.

"There you are," Seaforth sang out from a distance. "Miss Mitchell and I were wondering what could have detained you."

The lovely moment shattered, Regina's eyes flew open.

"Gina?" Constance called out, quickening her pace toward her cousin, "I could not think what might have detained you. Are you quite all right?"

No, I am not all right!

Regina was more disappointed than she would have thought possible at being deprived of her first kiss, and thoroughly ashamed of herself for the depth of her disappointment. She was grateful when Lord Harcourt finished straightening the veil and stepped away, leaving her shielded from prying eyes.

As for his lordship, he greeted Lieutenant Seaforth calmly, and with apparent pleasure, almost as though nothing out of the ordinary had happened. "We have arrived at last," he said, taking Regina's elbow and leading her toward the waiting couple. "A splendid estate, is it not?"

"Beautiful," Constance agreed.

"The gardens are up there," Seaforth said, indicating a terraced area reached by way of a flight of stairs. "Miss Mitchell and I took a quick peek before you arrived."

The dozen or so steps were actually squares of roughly cut granite, with the stones set into the earth in such a way that they appeared to have been not man's design but nature's. And though they were as handsome as they were dramatic, they looked rather treacherous.

"Is there another route?" Harcourt asked, "one suitable for ladies?"

Seaforth shook his head. "This is the only way open to the public. But there is no reason to be concerned, for the steps look more formidable than they really are. Miss Mitchell had not the least difficulty climbing them."

"If that is the case," Harcourt said politely, making Regina a courtly bow, "after you, Mrs. Farrington."

His manner was impersonal, like that of an affable host—no more, no less—and Regina wondered how he could appear so calm, when her own heart still thumped with the force of a blacksmith's hammer pounding the anvil. How could he act as though nothing had happened between them, when less than a minute ago he had been about to kiss her?

Of course, it was quite possible that the experience would not have been so very uncommon for him. Joel Harcourt was a handsome man, tall and strong, and in addition to his title, he had been further endowed with a knee-weakening measure of animal magnetism.

Blessed with more than his share of masculine attributes, he had probably kissed dozens of women before today. Perhaps even hundreds!

Hundreds?

Regina's heart slowed to its normal pace. How lowering to realize that if Lord Harcourt had kissed her, she would have been but one of many to him.

As they climbed the stairs, his hand beneath her elbow, the pressure no more intimate than might be expected of a hotel porter offering assistance, another possibility occurred to Regina, and this one was even more lowering than the last. What if Harcourt had not meant to kiss her at all? Intoxicated by his nearness and the light flirtation they had enjoyed during the last few miles of their journey, might she have imagined the whole?

Mortified by the suspicion that the entire incident had happened solely in her head—that the basis for its reality was a spinster's imagination—Regina spared a moment to be grateful for her concealing veil. Hid among the enveloping silk folds, her only consolation was that no one—his lordship included—was privy to her embarrassment.

While Regina bore her private shame, wishing she was back at The Knight's Arms with Felicity, that young damsel stood at the window of the suite, her telescope trained upon the distant channel, wishing she was any place other than the inn, restricted once again to those four walls.

Heartily sick of her own company, and bored to distraction with watching the endless waves wash upon the shingle beach, she turned away readily when a knock sounded upon the suite door. Expecting it to be one of the porters with the dinner menu, she was startled to find Mr. Oliver Drayson standing in the corridor, a small nosegay of violets in his hand.

"Mr. Drayson," she said, not hiding her pleasure at seeing him. "Good afternoon, sir."

"Good afternoon," he said, his face turning poppy red at the unexpected enthusiasm of her greeting. "Is your sister . . . Miss Mitchell, I should say . . . at home?" His face grew even redder. "Not *home*, of course. Know she is not there. What I mean to say, is she in the suite?"

"My sister is not here at the moment, sir. Was she expecting you to call?"

"No, no." The young gentleman shook his head, the

movement dislodging a lock of carefully combed hair that fell midway on his forehead. Glancing up through his pale eyebrows at the carrot-colored strand, he muttered something about cursing his luck.

"I beg your pardon?"

When Mr. Drayson sighed, and seemed unsure what to do next, Felicity asked if he would like to come inside.

"I shall be obliged to leave the door open, sir, for I am alone in the suite at the moment. The maid should return shortly, however, then I may offer you a cup of tea."

"No thank you," he replied. "I cannot stay. I have a gig outside. Rented it in hopes that Miss Mitchell might allow me to take her for a drive."

"What a shame that Constance is not here. If you return the gig immediately, is it possible to get your money back?"

He shrugged his shoulders. "I doubt it. Jobbers are real sticklers, don't you know. Strictly pay and play."

Unfamiliar with cant, Felicity had no idea what any of that meant. But it was enough for her ever-inventive mind that the gentleman before her had come prepared to go for a drive at the very moment *she* was in imminent danger of falling into a fit of the dismals from being forced to remain indoors.

With a rather bold idea taking hold of her thoughts, she sighed dramatically. "How I should adore a drive."

When he said nothing, she sighed again for good measure. "What joy to feel the sun's warmth upon one's face while the fresh sea air fills one's nostrils." She looked up at him then, her eyes wide. "Could anything be more felicitous?"

The young gentleman stared blankly at her.

"*Felicitous*," she repeated, smiling hopefully. "Have you forgotten my name?"

"Why, no, I . . ." Stopping short, he chuckled. "A good pun that. Jolly good. Sorry I did not see the connection immediately. Not usually such a slowtop, I assure you."

The laughter apparently having made him more relaxed, he handed over the nosegay. "Will you see Miss Mitchell gets these violets? And inform her that I brought them personally."

"Yes," Felicity replied, her tone dull, "I will convey your message."

"You will not forget?"

"No. I will put them beside the telescope, that way I will have no excuse to forget."

As though only just noticing the tripod and the handsome brass-banded telescope, Mr. Drayson entered the suite and made his way to the window. "I say! What a bang-up instrument. Whose is it?"

"Mine. I got it for my sixt—" She only just stopped herself in time. "What I mean to say, I got it last year."

Obviously, Mr. Drayson was too intrigued by the telescope to pay much attention to Felicity's near slip of the tongue. "May I?" he asked.

At her nod, he set his hat and driving gloves on the window seat and bent to look through the lens.

"Feel free to adjust it to your height, sir. I can readjust it this evening."

He looked at her then, as if seeing her for the first time. "You are interested in the stars?"

"The stars, the moon, the planets, the entire solar system."

Much struck by the fact that she even knew the term, he asked what she had seen.

"Mercury, Venus, Mars, and Jupiter," she answered without hesitation. "And a number of asteroids, of course. Not Saturn, however. Not yet."

"I have seen it with my telescope," he said. "But only once. I caught it out of the southwest just at sunset. It was last winter. And during that same week, I saw Venus and Jupiter seemingly so close they appeared to be almost touching."

"I saw that! I had read in the *Times* that it might happen, so I wheedled the gardener into constructing a simple platform for me out in the open. I stayed up all night with at least a dozen blankets wrapped around me for warmth."

"I also," he admitted, apparently happy to find a kindred spirit. "Wrapped up like a dashed worm in a cocoon."

They both laughed, then Felicity said, "I watched for so long, I feared I had gained a permanent crick in my neck. But it was worth the wait and the cold, for suddenly there they were in the eastern sky, just on the horizon. The brilliant Venus less than a degree south of Jupiter, the king of planets."

"Yes," he said, excited anew at the memory. "Could there be anything like it?"

She shook her head, though in agreement.

"Are we not living in marvelous times?" he continued. "Only think what Copernicus and Brahe, and Kepler would say if they were alive today!"

The two enthusiasts contemplated that awe-inspiring possibility in silence, then Felicity said, "Do you think they would be surprised to know about Uranus?"

"Rather! I am persuaded that even those geniuses never guessed there were *seven* planets."

They both sighed at the wonder of it, then suddenly Mr. Drayson recalled the hired gig waiting outside the inn. "About that drive, little one. I suppose there would be no harm in it. Would you care to bring your telescope? I know of a grand spot about three miles west of here, along the shoreline, where with a good lens, one ought to be able to see forever."

Unwilling to give him even a minute to change his mind, Felicity ran to the writing desk and began scribbling a brief note to Gina, informing her cousin that she was with Mr. Drayson.

"While I finish this," she said, "you dismantle the telescope. Then, as soon as I fetch my bonnet and pelisse, we can be on our way."

"Right you are," he said. Then, with a look not unlike that of a man caught in a whirlwind, he said, "By Jingo! For a youngster, you certainly know how to get things organized."

Not even the anticipation of *seeing forever* could dim the very real view that awaited Felicity when Oliver gave her his hand and helped her jump down from the gig. Spurred to recklessness by a feeling of freedom and a blue sky that seemed to stretch into infinity, she hurried across the springy turf. Ignoring the yellow blossomed gorse that snatched at the hem of her skirt, she stopped only just in time when the earth simply dropped away, as though it had been cleaved by the hand of an angry giant.

Gulping a breath of the fresh, briny air, Felicity stood at the edge of the precipice, feeling for one brief, giddy moment as though she were one with the sea birds, and that she might actually soar with impunity over the white chalk cliffs, to land unharmed on the bottle green waters below.

"Steady there," Oliver said, catching her arm and urging

her back a step or two. "The last I heard, little girls were not numbered among the winged species."

"No," Felicity agreed, still staring off into the vast chalky whiteness that seemed to stretch for miles both east and west. "But if it were possible to fly, I should wish to do so. Would not you?"

"Oh, yes. That and more. If I could, I should like to go to the—"

When he stopped abruptly, as if having revealed more than he intended, Felicity turned to look at him. "Where would you like to go, Oliver?"

He shook his head.

"Please," she said. "Tell me."

"You will think me insane."

"I will not. I promise."

She thought he meant not to answer, but when she seated herself on the moist green ground, then reached up and caught his hand, giving it a gentle tug, he sat down beside her, his manner if not totally relaxed, at least not too wary.

"Where?" she asked again.

She still held his hand, but he seemed not to notice.

"I should like," he said softly, "to travel to the stars."

"To Venus?"

"There first, of course, it being closest. But ultimately I should like to see with my own eye all seven planets."

Having revealed his dream, he looked not at her but at the hand whose delicate fingers were laced with his. Then he touched each of her fingertips in turn, giving each the name of his desired destination.

"First Venus," he said, tapping her thumb. "After that Mercury. Then I should double back past Earth and continue onward to Mars and Jupiter. At last," he said, touching her pinky, "I would see for myself the rings of Saturn."

"And Uranus?" she asked. "Surely you would not leave that star unexplored."

"No," he replied, smiling rather self-consciously. "I would see them all. Unfortunately, I ran out of fingers."

"Not to worry," she said, holding up her other hand. "I have five more you may use. But only if you will let me come along on your adventure."

He caught her free hand and used it to cross his heart. "Word of a gentleman, little one. When I explore this universe of ours, I vow I shall take no companion but you."

Felicity watched his serious gray eyes as he crossed his heart and made his promise, and in that moment, she fell hopelessly, passionately in love.

Chapter Six

"I cross my heart," Lieutenant Seaforth said, "I am not just saying it to please you. Blue has always been my favorite color."

"Mine as well," Constance said.

They sat in a rustic swing shaded by an arched grape trellis, the leaves on the vines grown so thick they formed a cozy bower perfectly suited to a young lady and gentleman desirous of a moment's privacy before rejoining Lord Harcourt and Regina.

"And your favorite flower, sir?"

Constance was caught up in this exchange of preferences not only because she found anything to do with Seaforth of genuine interest, but also because his likes and dislikes so often paralleled her own.

"You will think me unpardonably sentimental, Miss Mitchell, but I have a strong partiality for poppies. There is a field near my home where in summer the poppies form a thick scarlet blanket that must be seen to be believed.''

"I have seen them," she said. "Not that particular field, of course, but one very like it. I, too, love the simple flowers, especially after the rain, when the sun bursts through to dispel the clouds, and the flowers seem to know there is a stretch of fine weather ahead. I have noticed that the poppy, with its lovely crinkled petals, will stand tall, as if reaching up to embrace the sun's warmth, almost as if waiting for its kiss.''

"Yes," Seaforth said, though the word was so softly spoken Constance was not certain she had heard it. He was looking at her mouth. "Fortunate sun," he whispered.

Constance knew a bitter-sweet ache deep inside her chest. Fortunate, fortunate poppy! she thought.

Regina saw almost none of the celebrated gardens of Cuthbert House. She strolled beside a wall spilling over with tendrils of greenish white bryony and clematis. She walked through a little wild garden charmingly overgrown with yellow lady's slipper, blue and white rosmarinus, and windflowers. She strode beneath arbors entwined with roses of every species, and past beds of pink thrift and showy delphinium, even offering such comments upon the beauty and aroma as were required of her.

But she never really saw them.

Nor, for that matter, did she taste the several dishes set before her at the al fresco nuncheon, contenting herself, for the most part, with pushing bites of food from one side of her plate to the other.

While her companions remarked enthusiastically upon the tenderness of the ham, the crispness of the salad, and the sweetness of the strawberries served in bowls of heavy cream, she said nothing. And on those few occasions when she felt obliged to raise a forkful of food to her lips, so disinterested was she that those morsels might as well have been scythed from the grass upon which she sat.

Following the meal, she was plagued with mixed emotions as she allowed Lord Harcourt to help her into his curricle. She had no desire to spend another hour in the gentleman's company, yet if she wished to return to Brighton and The Knight's Arms, she knew the trip must be got through.

For the first quarter hour, as the bays settled into a steady pace, the occupants of the carriage rode along in comparative silence, with only occasional innocuous remarks from his lordship regarding Cuthbert House, followed by monosyllabic replies on Regina's part. She had just begun to relax, supposing the entire trip might continue in this manner, when a muttered oath suddenly shattered her illusions.

"Deuce take it! What is going on?"

"Going on?" she asked, feigning a calmness she did not feel. "I am certain I do not know what you mean, sir."

This time, he was not so careful to muffle the oath. "Do not be obtuse, Regina. You know exactly what I mean. From the moment we reached the Cuthbert estate, you barricaded yourself behind that blasted veil, as though you were under siege."

"I did no such thing."

Disconcerted that he had seen through her defensive strategy, yet unwilling to discuss the reason for her actions, she tried stalling tactics, hoping good manners would keep him from pursuing the subject further. "Barricade myself

indeed. Sheer fancy. Believe me, sir, if it seemed as though
I was . . .''

"Being rude?" he supplied when she paused.

Regina had the grace to blush, though, thankfully, it
went unnoticed beneath the silk.

"I thought we had made our peace," he continued.
"Was it something I said?"

"No."

"Something I did, perhaps?"

Regina wished he would desist. When he looked like
continuing, she took a page from Felicity's book. "I pray
you, sir, do not plague me, for I have the headache."

"Caught from your young cousin, no doubt."

The man had no compassion!

"It is an interesting phenomenon," he said, "how viru-
lent headaches can be. I have seen the ailment sweep
through a dull party in a matter of minutes, sending half
the ladies in the room in search of their beds."

His quickness at seeing through her excuse both embarrassed and angered her. "Could it be, sir, that you are a
carrier? I have observed that those who do not know when
to leave well-enough alone often bring the disease with
them."

Unaccustomed to letting irritations lead her to act impul-
sively, Regina repined her own rudeness and was about to
ask his pardon when she noticed that he was having a
difficult time controlling his mouth. The corners twitched
as if he were fighting laughter.

"As you say, madam, I may be a carrier of the headache,
but I am persuaded your waspishness must fell an equal
number of unsuspecting innocents."

At first Regina could not believe he had uttered such a
remark, then her basic honesty rose to the fore and she

was forced to smother a chuckle. "Have a care how you choose to censure me, sir, for I have it on good authority that that particular insect numbers among its kind one or two males as well."

"To be sure," he said so affably Regina was hard pressed not to laugh aloud.

Aware of her difficulty, he turned upon her a smile so devastating it caused her to forget everything save the still balmy afternoon and the pleasure she derived from gazing upon his handsome countenance.

"I wish you would discard that blasted veil," he said. "If I am to exchange insults with a lady, I should like to see the expression on her face."

"As you wish, my lord."

As easily as that, she complied, lifting the silk and letting it fall where it would behind her head.

"Now that you have dispensed with that abomination, do you suppose we might dispense with my title as well? My name is Joel. May I hear it upon your lips?"

Regina's heart danced within her bosom. In all her twenty-six years, no gentleman had ever asked her to call him by his name. Certainly none had ever expressed a desire to hear his name upon her lips.

Joel.

After several moments, when she still had not spoken, his lordship, said, "While we are on the subject of lips, perhaps it is appropriate that we discuss what happened at Cuthbert House. And before we go through another round of denials, let me be blunt. I refer to the incident that made you feel it necessary to distance yourself from me."

No! He could not mean to bring that up. Not now. Not when she had only just regained her ease in his company.

The heat in Regina's face told her he could not be unaware of her embarrassment. Still, he continued upon his chosen course.

"Because you are a married woman, and acquainted with those attractions existing between the sexes, I do not scruple to mention what passed between us when I replaced your veil."

Attractions existing between the sexes?

Much too discomfited by what that phrase might mean, Regina was unable to look at him. Instead, she clasped her hands together in her lap, concentrating upon the dark netting of her gloves. "Please, I do not wish to discuss—"

"I had hoped to pass the incident off as a misunderstanding, but I should have known better. A woman always knows when a man desires to kiss her."

Regina felt her heart skip a beat. Had he truly said what she thought he said—that he had wanted to kiss her?

"Not that I fault myself entirely, madam. After all, what man with blood in his veins would not want to taste your lips?"

Her lungs must have forgotten how to perform their function, for she could not seem to draw sufficient breath.

"I make you no apologies for my feelings, Regina, for you are a beautiful woman. Very beautiful. But be that as it may, I want you to know that you need feel no reservations about being in my company. Do not fear that I will take liberties, for I do not kiss other men's wives."

So concentrated were Regina's thoughts upon his lordship's revelation regarding his wish to kiss her, and that he thought her beautiful—nay, very beautiful—that it was much later that evening before she recalled his concluding words. *I never kiss other men's wives.*

"An odd mistake," she said as she climbed into her virginal bed. "Surely he meant *widow.*"

"Damn the woman!" Joel muttered. Flinging himself into one of a pair of chintz-covered chairs that flanked the bedchamber window, he yanked at his cravat, then tossed the hapless cloth upon the topmost of a set of range tables.

"I am sure," his valet said, retrieving the crushed linen, "that Mrs. Drayson meant the dinner invitation in the spirit of family unity. But if you should wish to make your excuses, m'lord, I can send one of the inn porters 'round to the Royal Crescent with a message for your aunt."

"No, no. I shall dine with Aunt Trixie. For now, however, I am in the devil of a mood. Since my temper has nothing to do with you, you may wish to play least in sight."

The servant's calm demeanor never faltered. "Yes, m'lord," he said, then he bowed respectfully and strolled leisurely toward the door. "I shall return in an hour's time."

As soon as the door clicked softly behind the gentleman's gentleman, Joel gave vent to a most ungentlemanlike string of words, the last of which was accompanied by a boot that was thrown across the room to land with a thud against the heavy oak washstand.

Ever since he had bade Regina goodbye at the entrance to The Knight's Arms, and heard the breathless quality of her own words of farewell—an interesting sound that from any other women he would have taken as encouragement—Joel had been trying to rid his brain of a most unwanted vision.

In that vision, he stood upon a mist-shrouded dueling field. In his hand was a smoking pistol while at his feet lay the still-warm corpse of Regina's husband, the unknown Mr. Farrington. "Madam!" he shouted to the veiled figure who stood in the distance, "you have driven me to murder."

The other boot sailed across the room to join its mate, crashing against the washstand with such force it threatened to topple Joel's tin of tooth powder and his shaving mug.

"Damnation, Regina. Why could you not have been a widow in earnest? Or at the very least a crone, all shriveled and ugly."

No. Regina Farrington was much too uncooperative for that.

She was the most beautiful woman he had ever known, and from the first moment he saw her, she had not left his thoughts. So, of course, it must follow that she was not only still married, but also actively searching for her missing husband. Not dead. Missing.

Frustrated beyond endurance, he laid his head back against the chair cushion. "I am resolved to think of her no more."

Unfortunately, that resolution did not outlive the saying of it, for immediately he recalled that dreamy look in Regina's eyes when he had said she was beautiful. Almost as though she had never heard those words before. Heaven help him! How he had longed to take her in his arms and kiss her.

He pictured himself trailing gentle kisses all over her face, starting at her earlobe, then continuing across her satiny cheeks until he reached her soft mouth. He imagined his lips teasing, testing, tasting until they learned every facet of her lips; then he saw himself very still, his senses alive while she reciprocated, learning every facet of his lips.

He imagined—

"Harcourt?"

Joel sat up quickly, both angry and relieved at the interruption.

"Oliver," he said, with what he hoped was a hospitable voice. "What brings you here? I was scheduled to dine with Aunt Trixie in less than two hours. I trust you have not come to inform me that she has cancelled."

"No. Nothing like that. I merely thought we might talk. Man to man, as it were."

"Of course. Please," Joel said, motioning toward the chair that was companion to his own, "sit down. Make yourself comfortable. What is it you wished to discuss?"

Though his cousin sat down, he did not relax. Instead, he leaned forward, his elbows on his knees, his hands clasped before him. "What think you of Miss Mitchell?" he asked, getting right to the point.

Aware that it behooved him to tread warily, Joel stated the obvious. "Constance Mitchell is one of the most beautiful females I have ever seen. Why do you ask?"

Oliver hesitated. "I think I have fallen in love with the lady."

Joel tried to maintain a disinterested air. After all, this was part and parcel of why his aunt had asked him to come to Brighton, to keep her son from making a mistake that would ruin his life

"You only *think* you love her? You are not convinced of your feelings?"

"Yes, yes. Of course I am. Who would not love her? For she is an angel."

"Only . . ." Joel prompted.

"Only I have never been in love before, so I am not quite certain how it should feel. I thought perhaps you might tell me."

"Me?" Joel shook his head. "When it comes to the finer feelings, lad, I fear I am as much a novice as you. Now if it was lust you wished to know about, or any of the other not-so-finer emotions, I am acquainted with those all too well."

Oliver sighed, and Joel realized the young man was disappointed in both the answer and in his older cousin. "What makes you think you might be in love with the lady?" he asked.

"As you say, she is unbelievably beautiful, but it is not that alone. It is something that happened this afternoon when I went to call upon her at her suite."

"You were at The Knight's Arms? Today?"

"Yes. Only Miss Mitchell was from home. And when Felicity told me her sister had gone for a drive in the country with some chap in a cavalry uniform, I was quite jealous. So jealous, in fact, that I wished I could plant the fellow a facer and watch him fall to the ground at my feet."

Joel only just managed to hide his smile. "Well, sir, I would say that is proof of your jealousy, right enough. If it is any consolation to you, the number of men who have experienced that emotion are legion. However, I cannot vouch for jealousy being a proof of love."

While Oliver contemplated that piece of wisdom, Joel asked him a question whose answer *he* thought of interest. "How is it you heard of Miss Mitchell's outing from her sister? I thought that young miss was laid upon her bed with the headache."

"A headache? Felicity? Not her. She is too game a girl

for such missishness as that. Pluck to the backbone, the little star gazer.''

Instantly warming to the subject, the young man leaned back in his chair, relaxing for the first time since entering the room. ''You won't believe this, Harcourt, but Felicity is interested in astronomy. And not just interested. She is informed on the subject. Knows almost as much about the galaxy as I do.'' He smiled in remembrance. ''Lord, we must have talked for hours.''

''Did you now? It appears I was misinformed about that headache. May I inquire if you and the young lady had this long discussion of things astronomical in the suite?''

''No. We took her telescope to the cliffs west of the village. What a jolly time we had drawing star maps and plotting a course for—''

His cousin paused then, his face flushed, and Joel was immediately curious as to what they had done that the lad wished to keep private.

''Are you quite certain, Oliver, that it is Miss Mitchell you may have formed a tendre for? Or is it her young sister?''

Instantly angry, Oliver turned so red Joel feared the lad might explode. ''Cousin! I cannot credit that you even suggested such a thing. Why, Felicity is a little girl.''

''She is petite. I will give you that.''

Oliver's jaw was rigid. ''She is also a sweet and charming child.''

''She is definitely a charmer,'' Joel agreed. ''A charming minx.''

It was not to be wondered at that Mr. Oliver Drayson spared fewer than a dozen words for his cousin during

dinner that evening. It was Joel's belief that if his Aunt
Trixie had not been present, the irate lad might have been
tempted to plant *him* a facer. Good.

Joel still had no idea what the three young women were
up to. True, they had come to Brighton like a trio of players
acting parts, but he had no proof that their motives were
of the havey-cavey variety. Still, if his cousin was determined
to form an attachment for one of the sisters, Miss Felicity
was much more suitable for the office.

"So, Harcourt," Beatrix Drayson said once Oliver had
claimed a prior engagement with an old school chum and
quit the room, "you have met the object of my son's infatuation, this Mitchell creature. What think you of the
female?"

"Quite frankly, Aunt Trixie, I think you are worried over
nothing. I was in the company of Miss Mitchell and her
chaperone for the better part of the day, and unless I have
mistaken the matter, I believe the beauty is in a fair way
of giving her heart to an acquaintance of mine, a young
lieutenant."

His aunt placed her hand over her plump bosom, tears
of joy in her eyes. "Heaven be praised! A lieutenant, you
say. Oh, my boy, what happy news. How can I ever thank
you?"

He held up his hand to stem her enthusiasm. "It is none
of it certain, Aunt. As I said, I could be mistaken. However,
if you would oblige me in a small matter, one that would
not seriously tax your injured toe, perhaps we might both
discover that which we wish to know."

"I shall do anything, my boy. You have only to ask."

"I should like you to give a dinner party tomorrow evening."

"A dinner party, but—"

"I would have you send a card of invitation for this party to Lieutenant Wesley Seaforth, whose temporary residence is the Old Ship."

"As you will, nephew. And to whom shall I send the other cards?

"Dearest Aunt, in addition to the gentleman, I wish you to invite both the misses Mitchell and their chaperone, Mrs. Farrington."

Chapter Seven

If Joel's aunt was surprised to find herself giving a dinner party for persons she had previously suspected of having designs upon her beloved son, the guests were no less surprised to find themselves invited to the Royal Crescent.

"Famous!" Felicity said.

She had only just closed the suite door after relieving the porter of the missive he bore on a silver salver, and as she crossed to the loo table to hand the neatly lettered vellum to Regina, she noticed that three names had been printed there, hers among them. Snatching the invitation back, she held it to her bosom as if it were a prize beyond price.

"It has my name on it as well," she said in answer to Regina's unasked question. What she did not add was that she had also spied the letter *D* stamped in the sealing wax. "Since it is only my second invitation, if neither of you have an objection, I should like to open it."

Prior to Felicity's odd behavior, neither Constance nor Regina had shown the least interest in what they assumed was just one more invitation; after all, Constance had received dozens of requests for her company since arriving in Brighton. Now, however, they gave Felicity their full attention, waiting while she carefully broke the seal.

"It is from Mrs. Beatrix Drayson," she said, going directly to the signature.

Regina and Constance spoke in unison, though the animation of their reactions varied greatly.

"Oliver's mother?" Constance asked quietly.

"Harcourt's aunt!" Regina gasped.

"Yes to both. Mrs. Drayson has been so kind as to invite us to join a small, impromptu dinner party tomorrow evening. Oliver, Lieutenant Seaforth, and Lord Harcourt complete the list of guests."

Once again, her relatives spoke as one.

"How delightful," Constance said, anticipation upon her face.

"Under no circumstance!" Regina said, dismay writ upon her countenance.

It was her cousin's reply Felicity addressed. "You do not wish to attend? Why ever not?"

Regina's cheeks grew bright pink. "My . . . my veil," she said, as if clutching the first excuse that occurred to her. "It will be impossible to eat without removing it, so I . . . I cannot go."

Constance rushed to the loo table and caught her cousin's hand. "Please reconsider. I am persuaded it will be a lovely evening."

"Do not worry, Gina," Felicity said, "I am certain we can devise a plan that will allow you to be comfortable.

After all, you had reservations about going to Cuthbert Gardens. Remember? And look how well that turned out.''

As titular host of the dinner party, Oliver volunteered to fetch the young ladies in his mother's barouche. Joel and the lieutenant arrived first, having come in his lordship's curricle, and it was while they divested themselves of their hats that their host ushered in his charges.

If anyone was in any doubt as to Lieutenant Seaforth's sentiments, they had only to watch the bemused look upon his face as Miss Constance Mitchell entered the vestibule. He could not take his gaze from her.

She was breathtaking in a pale green dinner dress of gros de Naples, trimmed around the hem and at the sleeves with tiny rows of needlepoint lace. In keeping with the dictates of fashion for a young lady, her accessories were modest. Threaded through her blond locks was a simple green ribbon, and adorning her swanlike neck was a matching ribbon from which hung a gold, heart-shaped locket.

Joel bowed to her then watched as Seaforth possessed himself of her hand, tucking it inside his arm so that he might escort her to their hostess. On the alert, lest his cousin should decide to plant the lieutenant a facer, Joel was pleased to note that Oliver took his role as host seriously and was assisting Miss Felicity with her wrap.

As a matter of fact, that diminutive young lady was laughing at something Oliver had said, and he was gazing down at her as if well satisfied with his present companion. She, too, had threaded a ribbon through her light brown hair, and though her pale yellow dress was modestly cut, and suitable for a lady of tender years, to a gentleman of Joel's more advanced age and practiced eye, the slender form beneath the pale yellow silk appeared decidedly more mature than it had just the day before.

Apparently he was the only one to note the subtle change in the young lady's anatomy, for his cousin was even then giving himself the pleasure of examining the gold chain around her neck. With the familiarity of an old friend, he lifted the chain from which was suspended a number of gold charms, astronomical in shape, examining the moon and several stars.

"Capital!" Oliver observed. Then, counting the stars, he said, "But you have only six."

"I used to get a new charm each birthday," she said. "From my mother."

"But you must have the complete solar system. When is your birthday, little one? I insist you allow me the pleasure of giving you Saturn."

Joel failed to hear her reply, for he was on the alert for Regina's entrance. Since a heavy veil was totally inappropriate for a dinner party, he was curious to see what she had worn for the occasion. When several seconds passed and she had not joined them in the vestibule, he knew she had found some excuse not to come.

"Where is Mrs. Farrington?" he asked.

Felicity looked at him then, the expression on her pixie's face so innocent it made him suspicious. "My cousin bid me to make her excuses, my lord, for she is unwell this evening."

Joel raised a skeptical eyebrow. "Let me guess the nature of her malady. The headache?"

"Sir," replied the cheeky miss, only just suppressing a grin, "you are very astute."

* * *

Dinner was a pleasant enough affair, one rendered all the more relaxed by their hostess's obvious relief that her son was not hanging on Miss Constance Mitchell's every word. As for the saucy minx who made Oliver so forget himself as to laugh out loud several times during the meal, that damsel was too young to concern the gentleman's mother. Not only that, she was also, as Beatrix Drayson confided later, a very pretty behaved child, and as guileless as the birds in the sky.

Thankfully, Joel was not privy to that particular assessment until several days later, for the instant the meal was completed, and the guests adjourned to the second-floor drawing room for the pleasure of hearing Miss Mitchell perform upon the pianoforte, he excused himself to his hostess and went in search of the widow Farrington.

When Regina answered his knock, opening the suite door but an inch so she might look out, he dispensed with any pretense at formality. "Coward!" he said by way of greeting.

"Lord Harcourt! Why are you here?"

"I might ask you the same question, madam. And, please, do not give me a catalog of your spurious maladies. We both know why you did not accept my aunt's invitation."

When she vouchsafed no reply, he pushed the door all the way open, stepped past her, and entered the room. "Yes, thank you," he said, "I should be delighted to come in."

It was as he had suspected, Regina had not opened the door because she had not had time to fetch her veil. What he had not been prepared for was the jolt he received, like a flush hit to the solar plexus, when he saw her dressed in something other than the usual widow's garb.

She wore a simple muslin frock cut along classical lines, with a pattern of lilac flowers in the foreground and a deep purple ribbon tied just beneath her pretty bosom. As well, her hair was no longer confined in its usual chignon; instead, it fell free as a young girl's down her back, the long, wavy tresses flowing like water on a dark, moonless night.

While Joel looked his fill of her, unable to stop himself, he could not discern what set his blood to racing first. Was it the fresh, youthful look of her that had been eclipsed by the unrelieved black? Was it the sight of her slender figure—a figure that was as graceful as it was exciting? Or could it be the almost overpowering desire he felt to catch her close to him and bury his face in that glorious hair?

"Was this your sole purpose in pushing your way into my suite," she asked, "to stare rudely at me?"

Damn, but he loved her fighting spirit!

"I did not come for that purpose, Regina, but I cannot say I disliked being diverted by the sight of you in colors."

Regina could readily understand the concept of being diverted by an unexpected sight, for she had been hard pressed not to make a fool of herself when she first spied Joel. Dressed in a beautifully cut evening coat of mulberry, a waistcoat of purest white, and breeches that showed his muscular legs to advantage, he had never looked more handsome, nor more elegant—every inch the wealthy peer.

Suddenly shy of this prepossessing personage, she returned to the settee where she had been sitting earlier and retrieved her sewing, giving the now-erratic stitches her undivided attention.

"May I be seated?" he asked.

At her nod, he placed his hat upon the loo table and settled himself on the matching settee opposite her, crossing one long leg over the other. His lordship did not bother to introduce any topic for conversation, and since Regina was still too surprised at his visit to think of anything sensible to say, they remained silent.

In time, the room grew so quiet Regina fancied she could hear the thread as she plied her needle and pulled the embroidery silk through the material. She might have thought herself alone had she not felt his eyes upon her, watching her, making her wish she had had the foresight to tie her hair back, or to don a more modest fichu.

When she could stand it no longer, she tossed the sewing aside and gave him stare for stare. This tactic, far from shattering his lordship's composure, made him laugh. "Forgive me," he said. "When I took it into my head to come to see you, I had not meant it quite so literally."

"You had a purpose, then?"

"I suppose I must have. Though to own the truth, that purpose seems to have slipped my mind."

When she asked him if his visit had anything to do with Mrs. Drayson's dinner party, he surprised her with a seeming non sequitur. "May I inquire if you brought any other clothes to Brighton? Not," he hurried to assure her, "that I find anything wanting in the frock you are wearing. I merely wish to know if you brought anything suitable for a ball."

She hesitated a moment, not certain she wanted to disclose to him the fact that she had brought her entire wardrobe, for he was sure to ask why she had done such a thing. Not wanting to admit that she no longer had a home, and that if she did not find her father, she might be homeless forever, she made her answer evasive. "I have a green satin."

"Green," he repeated softly, making the word sound almost seductive. "I shall look forward to seeing it."

He rose then and strode over to the loo table to retrieve his hat. "Until Monday, Regina."

He was beside the door before she gathered her wits enough to detain him. "Monday?" she said. "Has Constance an engagement I know nothing about? Something for which she requires a chaperone?"

He shrugged his broad shoulders. "I confess, my dear, that I neither know nor care what that young lady has planned. It is you I wish to take to the Midsummer Night's Ball."

Regina thought surely she must have misheard. "You know I cannot attend a ball."

"Monday," he repeated. "Nine of the clock. And show me no black silk, madam, or I shall be tempted to drag you to your bedchamber and dress you myself."

"Sir! You pass the line of what is pleas—"

"Yes, yes. Let us agree that I am totally without manners and have done with the subject once and for all."

Not waiting for a reply, he set his hat upon his head, opened the door, and stepped across the threshold. Regina thought he meant to depart on the instant, but he did not. As if aware that she watched him, he turned back and tipped his hat, a devilish smile playing upon his lips.

"Monday," he said. "On the dot of nine. Green satin. Or else."

* * *

To say that her entire weekend was fraught with indecision was to understate the matter. For two days, while the heavens dumped rain upon the town, Regina could think of nothing save his lordship's threat. She would not dignify his ultimatum by calling it an invitation.

A Midsummer Night's Ball. It was so tempting to say yes. But, no! She could not go.

How could she even consider such a ruinous course? She would be discovered, and the charade would have been for nothing. All Constance's chances would be lost. With three of their four weeks already behind them, Regina could not afford to risk everything at this point, for her cousins' futures depended upon Constance receiving an eligible offer for her hand.

Yet Regina had not been to a ball since she left her uncle's home five years ago, and to own the truth, she found the idea of going to a fancy dress party again quite bewitching. As for the thought of dancing with Joel Harcourt—possibly waltzing with him, her hand in his, his arm around her waist—that prospect left her positively light-headed.

By Monday morning, she still had not decided what was best to do, and as a result of her inner turmoil, she had a headache in earnest.

"I was wondering, miss," Bessie said after she had brought their breakfast and set the places at the loo table, "if I could have this evening off? One of the porters at the inn, Jem's his name, says there's all kinds of fun and frolics to be got up to tonight, it being Midsummer and all."

The maid was wide-eyed with anticipation. "Jem says it's like a fair in the streets, with booths and pie men, and fortune teller's and the like."

She paused for a moment, then added with a shy pride, "At last year's celebration, Jem won the gurning contest."

Regina could only stare. Had Bessie found love in Brighton? There could be no other explanation for a female exhibiting such pride in a man whose claim to distinction was having won a contest in which each competitor stuck his head through a horse collar and tried to pull the ugliest face.

"At midnight," Bessie continued, "there'll be a fireworks display at the water's edge, and there's some as believe if a lass gets a kiss at the stroke of twelve, she'll be a bride by Michaelmas."

Since that last remark was accompanied by a sigh, Regina felt it would be harsh beyond permission to deny the maid's request. "You may have the evening off," she said.

"Oh, thank you, miss. And no need to fret none over your green satin, for I'll have it pressed and ready in plenty of time."

Regina thought surely she had misunderstood. "What did you say?"

"Your ball gown, miss. It's down in the laundry room being sponged, on account of it being folded in the trunk for so long. But not to worry, I mean to press it myself. There'll be only one person as goes near that satin with a hot iron, and that'll be me."

"Wh-whatever do you mean? I made no such request of you."

"No, miss. 'Twas his lordship told me you'd be needing the gown seen to."

It was all Regina could do not to gasp. "Lord Harcourt?

But when? How? I cannot believe he had the effrontery to speak to you about such a matter.''

''Oh, it weren't him personal, miss. He sent his valet over Saturday afternoon with a message for me, instructing me to see to the green satin.''

Reaching into her apron pocket, Bessie withdrew a handkerchief that had been knotted at both ends to protect a meager collection of coins. After giving the little bundle a shake, she sighed contentedly at the metallic jingle. ''His lordship's man gave me a yellow boy for my trouble.

''Of course,'' she hurried to assure Regina, ''if only you'd told me you wanted the dress for the ball, I would have been happy to see to it without no largesse. But I never had a whole quid before. Leastways, not to spend on myself.''

The maid continued to rattle on about the coming festivities and the jolly time she meant to have, but Regina heard only the sound of her voice. The words were nothing more than a jumble inside her head. She understood nothing that was being said. How could she when her brain was in a whirl?

Lord Harcourt was forcing her hand. He must have known, even when she did not know it herself, that she would not see to the gown, then use the fact that it was not pressed as an excuse for not attending the ball. Now he had taken that pretext from her, and she was left with but one argument against going—the very real threat of being seen and recognized.

She dare not show her face. When all was said and done, that fact—and only that fact—kept her from giving in to her wish to spend Midsummer Night in Lord Harcourt's company. No, not Lord Harcourt, Joel.

Nothing would have given her greater pleasure than to occupy the day preparing herself for the evening. If only it were possible for her to go, Regina would order a hip bath brought to the room, along with cans and cans of steaming hot water. After she had soaked for at least an hour, she would rub scented lotion into her arms and shoulders so they would appear soft and smooth in the revealing satin. Then, once she donned her one pair of silk stockings and the silver sandals that went with the gown, she would beg Constance to style her hair in some exotic manner befitting the occasion.

"So then," Bessie said, rousing Regina from her dream of preparation and bringing her back to reality, "I slid the box under my bed so no one would know it was there."

Obviously expecting to be congratulated for her inventiveness, Bessie smiled hopefully.

"I beg your pardon," Regina said, "I fear I am guilty of wool gathering. What is it you were so clever as to hide beneath your bed?"

" 'Twas the box I was telling you about, miss. The one brought by his lordship's man. I'm to keep it safe in my room in the attic until time to bring it down to you. "

Almost as if she had received an epiphany, Regina sensed the significance of that box. "Did you look inside, Bessie? Do you know the contents?"

"Oh, yes, miss. 'Tis a hooded domino, wrapped in tissue paper to keep it from getting crushed. Gray satin, it is, and grand enough for a princess, with a dainty mask to match."

Chapter Eight

While Regina took refuge in her bedchamber, trying to decide what to do regarding the domino and the fact that Lord Harcourt had removed every last excuse she had for not accompanying him to the Midsummer Night's Ball, Constance invited her sister to join her for a mid-morning walk.

"The exercise will do us both good," she said, "for I am persuaded you must feel as much a sluggard as I do after the rain necessitated our being confined to the inn the entire weekend."

Felicity readily agreed to the outing. Happy to be afforded an opportunity to leave the suite, she magnanimously resisted the temptation to point out to her sister that she had spent *every* weekend since they came to Brighton within the confines of those walls. Instead, she kept her tongue between her teeth and merely fetched her bonnet. "Where shall we go?" she asked, once they exited the inn.

"Let me see," Constance said, as if pondering an important question. "What say you to a stroll along the Marine Parade?"

"Or better still," Felicity amended, "perhaps we might have a look in at one or two of the shops. I should truly enjoy seeing the latest bonnets."

"Bonnets?" Her sister blinked, and for a moment those blue eyes registered dismay. "The shops here are, uh, much too provincial to be of interest. I assure you, you will find them quite boring. We would do much better to go for a stroll."

Felicity could only stare. The shops in Brighton too provincial? What foolishness was this? Such sentiment might be justifiable coming from a grand dame accustomed to the modistes of London, but from two young ladies fresh from Burwish, the idea was absurd.

Having been reared just outside a village that boasted scarcely a half dozen businesses, she could think of nothing more *provincial* than the one-room combination milliner and seamstress shop that had enjoyed a twice-a-week visit from the Mitchell sisters for as long as the younger of the two could remember. However, she kept that observation to herself, especially when Constance linked arms with her and began leading her inexorably toward the crowded Parade.

Any resemblance between their purposeful walk and a *stroll* was purely coincidental, and if Felicity had any doubts as to the method in her sister's madness, those uncertainties were erased when she saw the tall, blond gentleman in the blue tunic. Lieutenant Seaforth leaned against the colonnade at the entrance to Baker's Library, for all the world as if waiting for someone. Immediately he spied them and hurried forward.

"Lieutenant Seaforth," Constance said, her voice a bit breathless. "Good day to you, sir."

After executing a most graceful bow, he lifted her hand to his lips. "Miss Mitchell. Miss Felicity. What a pleasure to see you."

"And what a surprise," Felicity replied.

Fortunately, no one noticed her sarcasm, and since people milled about everywhere—this being the hour for the fashionable to show themselves in either the Steine or the Parade—Seaforth offered an arm to each lady. "Lest we impede traffic," he said.

At Mrs. Drayson's dinner party, Felicity had been too caught up in her own joy at being with Oliver to spare any special notice for her sister's pleasure in the lieutenant's company. Now, however, she was free to observe the rather intense glances that passed between the handsome couple. She was accustomed to gentlemen showing marked attention toward her beautiful sister, but this was the first time the beauty had displayed a similar interest in a gentleman.

"Your sister-in-law," Constance began, "I know she was happy to see *you* on her birthday, for how could she not. But may I ask, was she pleased with her gift as well?"

"Quite pleased. Actually, she bid me thank you for your part in the selection of the book."

"She is most welcome, I assure you."

The gentleman cleared his throat, as if a bit uncertain of the reception of his next words. "As you may imagine, she asked me all manner of questions about you."

A pretty pink stole into Constance's cheeks. "How flattering, to be sure."

As if recalling that they were not alone, Seaforth turned to Felicity. "She inquired after you, as well."

"Kind of her," Felicity said.

"Yes," Constance added, "it was very kind of Mrs. Seaforth to show such an interest in us, for we are complete strangers to her."

"My sister-in-law wishes to rectify that situation, and she bid me, as well, to extend to both you ladies an invitation to come to Horsham once your stay in Brighton is finished. She is most eager to make your acquaintance."

The pink in her sister's cheeks went an even deeper shade, and she mumbled something Felicity did not quite hear. An interesting exchange. Such marked attention from the lieutenant's family must mean that he had given them reason to believe his intentions were serious regarding the young lady. From the besotted look upon Constance's face, it was apparent that her affections were most definitely engaged, a situation that relieved Felicity's mind.

Since the day she had discovered that she loved Oliver Drayson, Felicity had been holding her breath, afraid her beloved might decide to offer for her sister, and petrified that the beauty might accept. After all, Oliver had been one of Constance's swains almost from the moment they arrived in Brighton. Loving the gentleman as she did, Felicity knew it would break her heart to see her sister married to him.

Now, however, it appeared she could relax with regards to that matter. With Constance and Seaforth looking into one another's eyes at every opportunity, and sharing private smiles, almost as if they were alone, it was obvious they were in love.

"I was wondering," Seaforth said, bringing her attention

back to the moment, "if you ladies had given any thought to attending the Midsummer Night's festivities?"

To Felicity's certain knowledge, her sister had already turned down three unexceptionable invitations for the evening. However, she decided that some information was best kept to oneself, especially when she heard Constance say, "It does sound a most enjoyable event. Unfortunately, we have no one to escort us."

From the smile on Seaforth's face, that was the answer he had hoped to hear. "If I may be so bold, Miss Mitchell, may I be permitted to escort you?"

That evening, the rooms at the Castle Inn were decorated to resemble a sylvan glade, with pots of greenery filling every corner and each of the window embrasures while garlands of fragrant sweet lilies—their stark white trumpets interspersed with yellows, brilliant scarlets, and purples—festooned the chandeliers and the paintings of Cupid and Psyche. As well, the flames of hundreds of candles lit the rooms, adding measurably to both the fragrance and the heat.

Regina noticed only the beauty. For her, the rooms were a wonderland worthy of Titania and Oberon, the king and queen of the fairies.

Befitting the occasion, at least a dozen of the ladies present had chosen gowns of filmy gauze to emulate Titania, and fully twice that many had chosen to don dominos and masks.

"Will you be brave?" Joel asked, "and allow me to divest you of your newest disguise?"

For just an instant, Regina hesitated; then logic convinced her that no one viewing her at that moment could possibly associate her with the veiled figure they had become accustomed to seeing as Constance Mitchell's chaperone.

She reached up and untied the ribbons of her mask, being careful not to disturb the cascade of ringlets her cousin had fashioned so cunningly, with one lone curl caressing her neck. Meanwhile, Joel took it upon himself to release the clasp that held her domino.

"Here," he said, signaling to one of the waiters, then slipping the gray satin from her shoulders. Only after he had handed over the cape and mask to the servant did he get his first real look at the lady he had escorted to the ball.

The widening of his brown eyes, plus his quick intake of breath told Regina all she needed to know, but it was balm to her heart when he took both her hands in his and leaned close to her so he might whisper in her ear. "On another occasion," he said, "you rebuked me for calling you my lovely colleen. With that fitting epithet denied me, I am left with no alternative but to inform you that I have never beheld a lady as beautiful as you."

Regina's heart seemed to stop beating for a time, but it was a small price to pay for the magic of such words— words she had thought never to hear. Having been denied a father's affection, she had never been told by a male that she was beautiful, not before tonight, and the tribute was doubly precious because it had come from Joel.

Not even trying to hide her emotions, she looked up at him, allowing whatever was discernible in her eyes to be so. "On this special occasion," she said, "in this fairy land, you may say anything you like to me."

The pressure of his hands increased, holding hers very tightly, but otherwise Joel's face was unreadable. He stood quite still, his brown eyes searching hers, and as he continued thus, an excitement grew in Regina—an awareness of the sheer masculinity of the man before her, and an awakening of a heretofore dormant yearning within her to know more of that masculine essence.

Still without speaking, he lifted her left hand and placed it on his upper arm, then slowly he slipped his arm around her waist, gathering her so close they were almost touching. Bemused by his nearness, Regina did not realize the significance of what he was doing, and he had already begun to twirl her around the floor before she assimilated the fact that the musicians had struck up a waltz.

Never having performed the dance in public before, she might have been tempted to look at her feet to make certain they obeyed the command of her brain, had Joel not exerted his own command. As if he knew her doubts, he held her firmly within the circle of his arm, leading her in the graceful bend and swirl of the four-four time until the rhythm became a part of her beating heart.

Surrendering to the beauty of the music and the mesmerizing effect of following Joel's masterful, yet gentle lead, Regina felt she could continue waltzing forever.

It was not to be expected that the musicians would share her sentiments, and in due time the waltz came to an end. However, there were any number of country dances to be enjoyed, and Regina danced them all.

Owing to the relaxed atmosphere of Midsummer Night, a flattering number of gentlemen asked if they might lead her in a set—gentlemen she knew well from her three-week sojourn in Brighton, but who had no idea that they had ever met her before.

"If the lady is willing," Joel informed the applicants, "I

will allow the dance. But as for making introductions, under no circumstances will I perform that office."

Her anonymity thus safeguarded, Regina was forced to hide her laughter more than once when faced with flirtatious gambits aimed at discovering her identity.

"Pray, tell me your name, fair enchantress," a gentleman who had paid court to Constance importuned. Naturally, Regina refused to enlighten him. Nor was she any more cooperative when another of her partners insisted they could not have met before. "Believe me, my emerald goddess, I would have remembered a creature as lovely as you."

She neither sought nor enjoyed such flattery, and though she was unfailingly polite to the half dozen men she stood up with, Regina found their company sadly flat after the exhilaration of being with Joel. As for her escort, he danced with no other lady. While Regina was engaged, he chose instead to find some vantage point from which he could watch her. Far from disturbing her, his constant vigilance lifted her spirits, and if it would not have caused a scandal, Regina would have refused other partners entirely and danced every set with Lord Harcourt.

When the musicians left the dais at eleven, and the couples began making their way toward the supper room, Joel asked if she had any objection to a stroll down to the shore.

"No objection at all. Actually, I should like to see the fireworks display."

"Then let us waste no more time in discussion," he said, "for I believe the display is scheduled for midnight. If we leave now, perhaps all the choice viewing spots will not be taken."

Regina fetched her domino from the ladies' cloak room,

and in less than five minutes she and Lord Harcourt were strolling down the Steine, the Prince Regent's fantastic Chinese Pavilion behind them. The domed white structure was alight with thousands of candles, and faint strains from a string quartet could be heard, but Joel and Regina, caring no more for Prinny's party than for the one they had just left, continued on their way toward the Marine Parade.

As they trod the rough streets, Joel gave it as his opinion that the cobbles might prove tricky beneath her silver sandals. To insure that Regina did not stumble, he took her hand and tucked it securely in the crook of his arm, pinning her wrist snugly against his side.

Her breathing accelerated by the novel experience of a rock-hard arm beneath her hand, Regina searched for something to say. "Lieutenant Seaforth agreed to escort Constance and Felicity to the celebration. Perhaps we shall meet them there."

"For Seaforth's sake," Joel said, a teasing light in his eyes, "I sincerely hope not, for then I should be obliged to shoot him and toss his body into the sea. I have shared you with enough gentlemen for one evening. More than enough, actually, and my patience is at an end."

Though she chuckled at his threat of violence, Regina was gratified to know that Joel wanted to be alone with her, and she gave herself up to the enjoyment of being alone with him. Or as alone as two people could be when traversing the center of a village where several hundred boisterous merrymakers were caught up in the festivities of the longest day of the year.

The Midsummer twilight had finally given over to night, and torches were being lit all along the Marine Parade and the cliff walk, where dozens of booths had been set up by local inhabitants for the sale of food, crafts, and drink. The thick, tangy aroma of meat pies wafted through the air as did the sweet, spicy scent of cider and the pungent smell of homebrew. From the unusual camaraderie and good cheer exhibited by many of the celebrants, it was obvious that those who manned the drink booths were experiencing no lack of customers.

"Ned!" yelled one old seaman who stood beside one of the hastily constructed stalls. "Come wet your whistle, lad."

"Don't care if I do," replied the other, staggering toward his friend.

Similar reunions took place at the next stall, and as the throng of revelers increased their consumption of ale, they began to call for music and dancing. From strolling troubadours seeking small donations for their performances, to local lads piping a tune on homemade whistles, music was never far away.

Only let a few notes sound, and the dancers gathered round as if conjured up by magicians. While little children skipped ring-around-rosie, and young couples whirled in one another's arms, work-hardened fishermen linked elbows with their fellows and stomped their way through spirited reels, many singing at the tops of their lungs.

As Joel and Regina wound their way through the noisy crowds, he laid his hand over hers where it rested upon his arm. "On the chance that someone might think you in need of a partner," he said, giving her fingers a squeeze, "I mean to hold you fast. I did not leave the ballroom at the Castle Inn only to lose you to some jug-bitten fisherman who will likely spend the next two days nursing a sore head."

"Spoilsport," she teased. "For here was I, thinking what fun it would be to dance a reel."

"And here was I," he said, raising his voice over the din,

"thinking what a pleasure it would be to find a quiet spot where we could talk without being obliged to yell."

By common consent, they walked westward along the cliff wall toward the old battery where the canons were once positioned to protect the town from the French. When the crowds began to thin out, they found a spot along the waist-high stone parapet where they might stand to view the fireworks display without being shoulder to shoulder with other onlookers.

They had only just laid claim to their spot when the first explosion sounded and a burst of white light shattered the peaceful sky. The initial barrage was greeted by cheers and applause, then at each succeeding explosion, the crowd grew quieter, their reactions limited to gasps of wonder and hushed sighs. Bright blues, reds, and yellows rained down from the heavens, their luminous beauty magnified by their reflections in the waters of the channel.

Regina watched the vivid colors streaking across the heavens, her head leaned back in an attempt to take in the entire panorama. When she put a supporting hand at her nape, it seemed the most natural thing in the world for Joel to step behind her. Without a word, he wrapped his arms around her waist, pulling her close to him so that her head rested against his shoulder.

"To spare you getting a crick in your neck," he whispered in her ear.

The fireworks were all but forgotten as Regina felt the hardness of Joel's chest at her back and the strength of his arms holding her, embracing her. For a moment she remained perfectly still, then the warmth of his body permeated her cloak, and the heat it ignited inside her caused a languor that attacked her knees, weakening them and making it necessary for her to lean her entire weight against him.

Not at all dismayed by her need for support, Joel tightened his hold on her. When he leaned forward and rested his cheek against her temple, the colors that had once exploded in the sky were suddenly bursting inside Regina's heart, their brilliance coursing through her veins, making her aware of every inch of her body.

"You feel wonderful in my arms," he whispered. "Soft, and warm, and vibrant."

"I . . . I do?"

"Mm-hmm," he murmured.

They remained thus for the duration of the pyrotechnics, neither moving nor speaking.

In time, the final display was shot into the air, accompanied by a thunderous boom, then exploding into a rainbow of colors—colors that seemed suspended for a time, like thousands of stars just out of reach. When those heavenly illuminations began drifting down to earth, leaving trails of red and gold, blue and green, Joel put his hands on Regina's shoulders and gently turned her so she was facing him.

In the muted glow of the lights, he slipped his hands from her shoulders up to the sides of her neck, then further up to cradle her face, tilting her chin so he could look into her eyes. Green eyes became lost in brown as he asked his unspoken question.

In an instant the lights were gone, swallowed up in immeasurable darkness, and in the hush that followed, Regina felt Joel's warm breath upon her skin as he brought his head down. "Regina," he whispered. "My sweet, beautiful colleen."

His mouth covered hers, and Regina forgot all else;

forgot everything save Joel and the feel of his lips, firm yet gentle as they coaxed hers to respond.

The sound of applause and the shouts from the crowd cheering their appreciation for the fireworks signaled the end of the kiss. As Joel lifted his head, leaving Regina's lips exposed to the cool air, and making her long for him to bend close and warm her once again, a fiddler close by began to play a song.

It was a haunting tune, the notes soft as velvet. Before Regina realized what was happening, Joel caught her hands and placed them behind his neck, then he slipped his arms around her waist, lifting her several inches off the ground. Slowly, quietly he began to dance.

See Rome and die! the ancients had proclaimed. For Regina, gliding on air, locked in Joel's embrace, she thought those Romans had much better have said, *Dance with the man you love and die!*

Love?

At the very idea, her brain felt as if it might explode like the fireworks. Love? What folly was this? It was preposterous. It could not be.

Beware, she warned herself. In the semi-darkness, with the smell of the sea filling a person's senses, it was easy to get caught up in the Midsummer madness. Easy to mistake passion for something more.

After several turns, with Joel holding her so close she was certain she could feel the beat of his heart blending with her own, he finally set her back down and relaxed his hold. Unfortunately, by the time Regina's feet touched the cobbles once again, it was already too late. The damage had been done. The preposterous had become perfectly reasonable. Regina Farrington loved Joel Harcourt. Loved him with her heart, her soul, and her body.

That thought, with all its ramifications, caught her so completely off guard that she could not look at him. Her breathing grew erratic and she could barely swallow. How had this happened? When had it happened?

Regina was not some foolish young girl to be swept away by an evening's romantic enchantment. She was a woman, full grown, with a woman's knowledge of the world—a very practical world in which love and marriage did not always go hand in hand. If the truth be known, they seldom went hand in hand. Especially when the gentleman was a wealthy peer and the lady without funds or connections to recommend her.

Disturbed by the turn of her thoughts, Regina decided she could not remain in Joel's company another minute. "I must go home," she said. "Immediately, please. I am unwell."

On this occasion, Joel did not tease her regarding the nature of her ailment. He had no need to do so, for he knew all too well what had turned a wonderfully responsive woman into a skittish girl.

I never kiss other men's wives. Too late those words had penetrated his brain.

On their return from the gardens at Cuthbert House, he had assured Regina she need not fear that he would take liberties, stating as his reasons his scruples against kissing other men's wives. Yet here he was, holding her, kissing her, taking all manner of liberties, and imagining himself taking even more.

"Come," he said, his tone more brusque than he meant it to be. "I shall have you back at The Knight's Arms in a matter of minutes."

Ten minutes later, at the entrance to the inn, Joel bid Regina a brief farewell. She allowed him to kiss her hand, then as he watched, she pulled the domino's hood up to conceal her face, and hurried up the broad staircase that led to her suite.

"Damnation," he muttered as she disappeared from sight. "First thing tomorrow, I will return to North Street."

There was no help for it; he must go. He was determined to find out about Regina's husband, and to do so, he had need of the elusive Mr. Thom Newton.

Though Regina wanted nothing so much as the privacy of her own room, privacy in which to sort out her jumbled thoughts, she was not allowed that luxury. As soon as she entered the suite, dark save for the illumination of one small candle that stood on the writing desk, she became aware of muffled sobs. Looking around for the source of the morose sound, she spied Constance huddled in the window seat, her feet tucked beneath her and her face buried in her hands.

"My dear," she said, going to her cousin's side, "whatever is the matter? You sound as if your heart is broken."

After a series of sniffs, the beauty looked up. "It is," she replied. "And I shall never be happy again."

"But are you quite certain, my dear?"

"Quite," her cousin replied, availing herself once again of her sodden handkerchief.

The barrier of her usual reserve penetrated, Constance had spent the last twenty minutes telling Regina of her love for Lieutenant Seaforth and his for her.

"But if he made you an offer of his hand in marriage, I cannot see . . ." Regina stopped, happy for the shadows existing at the window seat. "It was an honorable offer, was it not?"

Constance gasped. "Of course it was honorable! How can you ask such a question? Wesley Seaforth is the most wonderful man in the entire world."

Taking her cousin's hand, Regina asked her pardon. "I cannot think what got into me. However, if he wishes to marry you, and you love him as much as you have declared—"

"I do love him. I adore him. And I will never love another."

"Then, my dear, I fear I cannot see what has caused you such distress."

Constance pulled her hand away. "I cannot marry Seaforth. Surely you must see that."

"I see nothing of the sort."

As if speaking to one lacking in basic intelligence, she said, "He is a second son and has no fortune of his own."

Regina could not believe she had heard correctly. "What folly is this?"

" 'Tis not folly, Gina. Indeed, the matter is quite serious. Seaforth's situation in life requires the strictest economy."

"Can I have so misread your character? You did not used to be so very interested in wealth. When did those considerations gain such particular importance in your sight?"

"They have not. Not for myself. If I needed to consider only my own feelings, I should be happy to share my life with Seaforth even if we were obliged to live in a crofter's cottage." She sighed. "If I were with the man I love, I should be quite happy to spend my days in homely pursuits, preparing meals, spinning cloth, tending the chickens."

Regina did not question her cousin's sincerity, though she took leave to doubt the necessity for the bleak picture Constance envisioned of her future in a one-room hovel.

"However," the broken hearted girl continued, "there are others to consider. Seaforth's brother may expect him to marry advantageously."

"I cannot think that is the case, my dear. The lieutenant did not appear to me to be on the lookout for a female possessed of a large dowry."

Though much struck with this logic, Constance would not allow it to distract her from her determined course. "And what of Felicity? While I might find life as a soldier's wife everything I ever wanted, how can I expect her to share such an existence?"

"Have you asked your sister's opinion on the subject?"

Constance shook her head. "Felicity does not know that Seaforth made me an offer. She went to bed early. It seems Mr. Drayson means to take her some place tomorrow morning. To one of the hills just above the village where they can make use of the telescope. He took the instrument with him this evening."

Regina had not even noticed the absence of Felicity's prized possession. "Mr. Drayson was here tonight?"

"We met him at the Midsummer Night's festivities, and when the crowds became too rowdy, Seaforth suggested we come home. Mr. Drayson and Felicity made their plans while we walked back to the inn."

Regina found this last bit of news encouraging.

"It is my belief," she said, "that your sister wants nothing so much as your happiness, and I cannot convince myself that she would wish you to make any sacrifices on her behalf. Therefore, if your happiness lies with Lieutenant Seaforth, I urge you to seize the opportunity while you may."

"But our purpose for coming to Brighton was so that I might find a rich husband."

"If I remember correctly, that was Felicity's plan, not yours."

"True. But I agreed to it. And now there are only five days left of our allotted time. Your money is spent, and if I do not marry a wealthy man, I will never be able to repay what we owe you."

"I beg of you, my dear, do not let that be a part of your consideration."

"But I must. The five hundred pounds was your legacy, Gina, and I should not have let Felicity badger you into spending it. If you should remain a spinster, you will have need of every penny to sustain you in your old age."

Finding that prospect daunting in the extreme, Regina decided not to dwell upon it. "Perhaps there is a solution to this dilemma. A solution that would not require you to reject Lieutenant Seaforth's offer."

Constance turned hopeful eyes toward her cousin.

"Have you forgotten," Regina asked, "that my search for my father continues? I have not given up hope of finding him. And who is to say what my situation may be once we are united."

She stood and helped her cousin to rise to her feet. "Promise me you will not cry another tear until I have had an opportunity to speak with Mr. Thom Newton."

"But when will that be? We have but five days remaining, and Mr. Newton seems destined never to return to his office."

"He must return some time," Regina declared, as much to lift her own spirits as those of her cousin. "I shall go to North Street first thing tomorrow and, if need be, take up residence there. I am determined to speak with Mr. Thom Newton, and I shall allow nothing or no one to stop me."

Chapter Nine

For a young lady hopelessly in love, rising before day-break for an assignation with the morning star and the gentleman who filled her heart was a pleasure not to be missed. Knowing that Oliver was belowstairs, and not wanting to miss a minute of his company, Felicity moved quickly, donning one of the ankle-length muslin dresses that was part of her youthful costume and tying her long hair back with a matching pink ribbon. Choosing to take her capote as protection against the morning air, she fastened the cape at her neck then pulled the hood over her head.

After closing the suite door soundlessly, she tiptoed down the stairs and let herself out the entrance to the inn. True to his word, Mr. Oliver Drayson stood just beyond the door, waiting to help her up into the rented gig.

Neither of them spoke until the horse had begun its *clip-clop* down the quiet, moonlit street, then Oliver turned and winked at Felicity. "You are prompt, little one."

"I strive always to be so, for I detest being detained for no other reason than another's disregard for time."

He laid his hand over hers. "My friend," he said, amusement in his voice, "if I discover just one more admirable quality in you, I shall be obliged to marry you out of hand. There is no help for it, for no matter how many years I must wait until you are all grown up, it is certain I shall never find a lady whose likes and dislikes so completely parallel my own."

Felicity turned her hand beneath his, lacing their fingers together. "For the record, Oliver, how grown up do you think I need be?"

He pretended to give the question his utmost concentration, putting his head at an angle as though that would help him think. "I am not up to snuff on such matters, you understand, but I believe my mother was not fully eighteen when she and my father were wed."

He laughed, then freed her hand so he could chuck her under the chin. "It is a mute point, however, for in all likelihood, once you have reached the marrying age, you will no doubt consider me an old codger. Or more importantly, by that time you will have caught the eye of at least a dozen dashing blades, any one of whom must be more interesting to a young lady than a fellow whose head is always in the sky."

Felicity would let no one disparage her beloved, not even the young man himself. "What care I for dashing blades, when I might be with a man who has promised to take me on a journey to the stars? Besides, you are the most interesting person I have ever met."

"Not at all," he said, his tone embarrassed. "I fear I am a rather dull chap, little one. Everyone says so."

"They had better not say so to me!"

At her championing, he raised her fingers to his lips. "What shall I do when I must return to Dray Manor? How I will miss you, my little friend."

Felicity's heart seemed to slam against her chest. "You are returning home? When?"

"In a matter of days. Friday, perhaps. We took the residence in the Royal Crescent for May and June only, and our lease is up at the end of the week."

Though her own stay at the inn was fast drawing to a close, somehow Felicity had never thought that Oliver might leave.

"Furthermore," he continued, "my mother wishes to be in her own home, and I cannot say I blame her. Except for the melancholy prospect of no longer sharing your company, I would be wishing myself at Dray already."

No! Do not wish yourself gone from me so soon.

Felicity could not bear the thought of being parted from Oliver. Or worse yet, of never seeing him again. Today was Tuesday, and he spoke of leaving on Friday.

"In four days," she said, the words a mere whisper.

Until that moment, she had not faced the reality of her situation. When they had come to Brighton in search of a husband for Constance, it had seemed the easiest course for Felicity to pretend to be younger than her actual age. No one had foreseen the possibility that the ruse might have unlooked-for consequences. No thought had been given to the possibility that she might lose her heart.

But she had lost it. She loved Oliver Drayson, and he believed her to be a child. His *little friend* he called her.

He would miss her company—he had said as much—but he was ready to be home. He would return to his own world, and it was a world in which Felicity had no part.

"Will you miss me?" he asked softly, gazing at her as though she were a favorite kitten.

Felicity could not answer. Not with him looking at her in a way that made a lump rise in her throat—a lump so painful she thought surely she must cry out in anguish.

"I know," he said, "that I shall miss you. More I think than I had realized."

Oliver is leaving.

As the words echoed inside Felicity's brain, the constriction in her throat threatened to choke her, and she turned her face away lest he see the unshed tears that were burning her eyes.

"Is something wrong?" he asked, breaking into her thoughts. "It is not like you to be so quiet."

She shook her head, then she buried her face in her hands.

"Little one," he said, putting his arm around her shoulders. "What has distressed you? Tell me."

Do not go! she wanted to say, but she could not. Denied the solace of the words, the tears came instead, spilling through her fingers to fall unheeded into her lap.

"My dear," he said, tightening his hold on her shoulders. "I beg you. Do not cry."

No more able to do as he asked than she was to ignore the dictates of her grieving heart, Felicity turned and pressed her face into his neck cloth, letting the tears flow as they would.

Lost in her sadness, she did not know when Oliver directed the horse off the main road, stopping in a pasture dotted here and there with sleeping sheep. She was aware of nothing save the fact that somehow both his arms were around her, and that he was entreating her to tell him what he must do to relieve her suffering.

"If I have hurt you," he said, "I shall never forgive myself."

"No, no. The blame is mine. All mine."

Oliver put his hand beneath her chin, applying gentle pressure so that she was obliged to look up at him.

"You? Blameworthy? Do not talk such fustian." Using the pads of his thumb to wipe the tears from her cheeks, he said, "You are as innocent as one of those lambs in the distance."

He was occupied in wiping her tears, all the while gazing deeply into her eyes, when suddenly he grew very still. He looked at her in a way he had never done before, almost as though seeing her for the first time, and something in his gaze robbed Felicity of all desire to cry.

When his hand cupped her face, then began stroking her cheek, as though he needed to feel the texture of her skin, she moistened her suddenly dry lips with the tip of her tongue. The unintentionally provocative gesture caused him to catch his breath, and in the next instant his lips were touching hers.

The kiss was everything Felicity had ever wanted. Warm and soft and so sweet she thought she must have gone to heaven.

"My angel," he whispered, his voice hoarse. "My sweet girl."

When he kissed her again, Felicity's heart very nearly burst for joy. "Oliver," she murmured, "I—"

"Felicity!"

The word was wrenched from him as he pulled away from her, shock making his face appear pale in the moonlight. "What have I done?"

Immediately, shock gave way to incredulity. Then just as quickly, incredulity yielded to disbelief. "This is insanity."

When Felicity reached out to touch him, he jumped from the gig as if needing to put sufficient distance between them.

"It is all right," she said. "I wanted you to kiss me."

"You do not know what you are saying. You are a child."

As though the very word accused him, he balled his hand into a fist and hit it against the side of the gig. "You have no idea how despicably I have acted. I should be horse whipped."

Unable to endure his torment, Felicity jumped from the gig. When she would have touched his arm, to beg him to allow her to explain, he spun about and walked some distance away, turning his back on her. "Stay there," he said. "Do not come near me. I am not a fit person for you to touch."

Knowing she must convince him he had nothing to reproach himself for, she unfastened her capote and let it fall to the ground. Next, she removed the concealing, cross-over fichu so that nothing marred the line of the simple, high-waisted dress she wore. Finally, she caught her long hair, twisted it around her hand, then wound it into a knot atop her head, tucking the ends in as securely as possible.

"Oliver," she said, stepping into a pool of light. "I wish you to do something for me."

His voice was hollow. "What would you have me do?"

"Turn around, please."

For a moment, she thought he meant to refuse, but finally he turned.

"Now," she said, "I want you to look at me. Really look at me."

For what seemed an eternity, he stared at her, then

slowly his expression changed from anguish to uncertainty. "Felicity, I do not understand. What does this mean?"

"It means," she replied, the words more difficult to say than she had thought possible, "that I have been playing a part. I am not a child, Oliver. I am but three years younger than Constance."

"Three years! But Miss Mitchell is—"

"My sister is twenty," she finished for him, "and I am seventeen years old."

He said nothing for a full minute, and when at last he spoke, his voice was tight with anger. "So. This was all a jest? You were making a May game of me. I trust you enjoyed your sport."

"It was not like that. We—"

"We? Are you telling me that your sister was part of this deception?" He breathed deeply, as if only just controlling his emotions. "In the evenings, did the two of you share a laugh at my expense?"

"Oliver, please allow me to relate to you the circumstances under which we came to Brighton, for then I am persuaded you will understand the need for—"

"I understand enough," he said. "What a buffoon I must have appeared."

"Never! You must believe me. It is not what you think. I would not—"

"Be so good as to climb into the gig, so that I may take you back to the inn."

"If you would give me but a moment, I could explain everything to your satisfac—"

"Get in the gig. Now!"

She did as he requested, but when she would have spoken again, he put his hand up, as if to command her silence.

"I have heard all I wish to hear from you," he said. "At this moment, and in the future."

After attempting to convince a broken-hearted Constance that she need not give up the man she loved, Regina had gone to her bedchamber to spend what remained of the night tossing and turning, wondering what she was to do about her feelings for Lord Harcourt. That she had not heard Felicity leave the suite, nor been aware of the girl's return less than an hour later, bore testimony to her preoccupation with her own predicament.

Try what she would to be sensible, her thoughts kept returning of their own accord to the kiss she had shared with Lord Harcourt. And not only the kiss—though that was momentous in the extreme—but also his words of endearment.

His sweet, beautiful colleen.

Such heart-stopping words. In their own way, they had stirred Regina's soul as surely as Joel's kiss had stirred her senses. And such a kiss. She had never suspected it would exert such power over her. Indeed, she had never dreamed it could be so warm, so wonderful to be in a man's arms, and to feel his lips upon hers, evoking magical sensations, magical responses. Though she could not credit that any such enchantment would have existed if the magician had been other than Joel Harcourt.

And yet, after the enchantment, after the magical moments in his arms, had come the harsh reality. Joel had kissed her and called her his sweet colleen, but he had not spoken of what was in his heart. Indeed, though Regina had felt impelled to admit, if only to herself, that she loved him, obviously he suffered from no similar constraints. If his heart was affected, he kept the information to himself.

And why should he not? He had made her no promises. At no time had he attempted to discover her sentiments, nor had he shown any particular wish to be the recipient of her regard.

He had flirted with her; yes. He had teased her; most definitely. He had said he wanted to be alone with her; that, too, was true. And he had kissed her—kissed her with a passion Regina had never known existed. But when presented with a perfect opportunity to say he loved her, he had not.

Nor was he likely to do so.

Regina was no fool. She knew that a man of Lord Harcourt's wealth and ease of address could look as high as he liked for a wife; if he did, indeed, wish to be wed. She also knew that when it came to females without fortune or consequence, men of rank did not usually think of permanent alliances.

Unfortunately, though Regina was not so unworldly as to expect an offer of his hand, neither was she the kind of person who could accept a carte blanche. Though she loved Joel, loved him with all her heart, and was prepared to love him through eternity, she wanted that same gift from him. She loved him too much to take anything less.

Because she was unprepared to be Joel's mistress, and because he was unlikely to ask her to be his wife, Regina resolved that it was best for her—best for her aching heart—if she stayed as far away as possible from Lord Harcourt. No matter what the inducements, she would accept no more invitations that would throw her into his company. Never again would she be alone with him, nor would she allow any repetition of their heretofore frequent *tête à tête.* And should she encounter him in some public place, she would accord him only those civilities due any gentleman.

She made that painful decision in the hours just before dawn, and the hopelessness of her situation filled her with immeasurable sadness and not a few tears. Those tears were only just lessening when she heard Bessie puttering around in the sitting room, setting the loo table for their breakfast.

Since the maid was humming a rather happy tune—a tune Regina recalled hearing more than once last evening, played by a trio of strolling troubadours—she concluded that at least one of the females who attended the Midsummer Night celebration had returned home happy.

Regina heard the rattle of a serving cart being wheeled into the sitting room. Though the pungent aroma of coffee, toast, and basted eggs were so unwelcome they very nearly persuaded her to pull the covers over her head, at least the arrival of the food hushed Bessie's happy song. For that, if for nothing else, Regina could be grateful. When one is already suffering from melancholy, nothing insures further despondency so readily as the sound of another's happiness.

After Bessie had knocked upon her bedchamber door for the third time, Regina could postpone the inevitable no longer. Quitting her bed with the greatest reluctance, she pressed a damp cloth to her puffy eyes, donned a plain lawn wrapper, and joined her cousins, though neither of those young ladies seemed particularly cheered by her sacrifice.

As it transpired, Regina need not have worried about the tell-tale signs of tears on her own cheeks, for Constance's fair skin was blotchy and her eyelids were swollen and red, giving testimony to that damsel's unhappy mood. As well, if Felicity, whom Regina had not expected to see, was one wit happier than her sister and her cousin, she disguised the fact well. Red eyes seemed to be the look of the day.

That Constance should appear so was not surprising— Regina knew the nature of the beauty's despondency— but she could not imagine what had taken the joy from her younger cousin's countenance.

After the gathering of the three lachrymose ladies— none of whom spoke a word—to partake of food which none of them even tasted, Regina decided she should waste no time in paying her visit to North Street. With that objective in mind, she slipped into her widow's garb and donned the heavy veil, resolving as she did so that she would see Mr. Thom Newton before the day was out. If the man was not in his little pigeonhole of an office this morning, she was prepared to make herself as comfortable as possible in the lone ladder-back chair that stood in the far corner, and wait.

North Street was busy with activity, surprisingly so when Joel considered the amount of ale consumed the night before by the Midsummer Night revelers. In addition to a few sore heads, those villagers who stayed late to watch the fireworks must have had a devil of a time leaving their beds this morning.

Still, the narrow street seemed filled with pedestrians scurrying in and out of shop doorways, and Joel was obliged to dodge an aproned baker's helper who balanced upon his head a basket overflowing with loaves of dark, crusty bread. "Beg pardon, y'r honor," the lad said, hurrying on his way.

Congratulating himself on that near miss, Joel was forced to step lively to avoid a collision with an angry lout pushing a barrow laden with old clothes, chipped crockery, and dented cook pots. "Bloody toffs," the fellow grumbled before pushing on, the wheels of his barrow squeaking their protest of the cobbled street.

Hoping these encounters were not a foreshadowing of things to come, Joel crossed to the far corner of North Street and opened the door with the painted sign affixed to the lintel. Upon entering the dull little office, he was pleased to see that both the scarred desks were occupied.

As before, Newton's nephew, Burt, sat at the smaller desk, his face as sour as ever, though not nearly so insolent. The probable cause for the young fellow's lack of impudence was the thin, ferret-faced little man who sat at the desk that abutted his.

Burt looked up from the papers he was copying only long enough to recognize Joel, then he returned his gaze, if not his attention, to his work.

"Thom Newton, at your service," said the little man who jumped to his feet, bowing in an obsequious manner that made Joel immediately distrustful. "How can I help you, sir?"

"I was here several days ago, six to be exact, and I spoke with your nephew. He informed me—"

"Yes, sir," Newton interrupted. "Burt told me you was here asking about a lady. Won't you be seated."

While Joel sat in the ladder-back chair, his beaver hat and gloves on his lap, Thom Newton ordered his nephew to take himself off. "But mind you stay within shouting distance. When the gentleman is finished with his business,

I want you right back at your desk. I'll not be paying for hours not worked.''

Grabbing up a leather cap from a peg on the wall, Burt strode none too happily from the room.

''Now,'' Newton said, taking his seat again, and training his small gray eyes upon Joel, ''what can I do for you, sir?''

''The lady I enquired about is looking for a military gentleman.''

''Yes, sir. Lieutenant Nigel Farrington.''

He looked Joel up and down, a sly, calculating gleam in his eyes. ''But them as hire Thom Newton, and pay good gelt for his services, have a right to expect privacy. I'm sure you understand, sir.''

''Of course.''

Rightly interpreting the remark as a bid for money, Joel reached inside his coat and withdrew a leather pocketbook, from which he removed a small stack of five pound notes. ''I have no intention of breaching the lady's privacy,'' he said, counting out three of the notes and placing them on the edge of the desk. ''Nor do I wish to interfere in the business arrangement she has with you. I merely wish to speak with Lieutenant Nigel Farrington before she does, to ascertain for myself if he is the right man.''

''Of course,'' Newton repeated, not reaching for the money.

Joel counted out two more of the five pound notes and placed them on top of the stack. ''The world is filled with charlatans. One cannot be too careful where a lady is concerned.''

''No, sir,'' Newton replied, reaching across the desk and grabbing up the twenty-five pounds. ''A body can't never be too careful.'' He tapped his forefinger against his temple.

"That's why I keep everything here in my *nous* box where it's safe from prying eyes.

"However," he continued, stuffing the money inside the drawer of his desk, then locking the drawer with a key, "I know a gentleman when I meet one, sir, and I can see for myself that I don't have to worry none about your motives being dishonorable."

Having said this, he found a scrap of paper, flipped open the cap on a glass ink pot, and dipped a quill in the murky liquid. Hastily he scribbled something on the paper.

"This here," he said, "is where you can find Colonel Sir Nigel Farrington."

Newton waved the paper back and forth until the ink was dry, then he handed it across the desk.

"*Sir* Nigel?" Joel said, studying the scrawled direction. "Are you quite sure this is the man the lady is searching for?"

Newton took the question in good part. "I can't make no guaranties, mind you, but near as I can say, this Sir Nigel Farrington is the same soldier as married Miss Anne Regina Mitchell, of Byrn Park, near Burwish in East Sussex."

Chapter Ten

Regina walked with purpose toward the office on the corner of North Street, and as she passed a tobacconist's shop, she heard someone call her name. Though unaccustomed to being hailed on the street, she stopped and waited, only to be approached by the surly young man from Thom Newton's office. Not bothering to remove his cap, he stared rudely at her, as though attempting to see beyond her veil.

"It is Mrs. Farrington?"

"It is."

"You got business wif me uncle?"

Choosing not to give the insolent puppy the lesson in manners he so richly deserved, Regina said, "Is Mr. Newton in the office today?"

" 'E's there, right enough, but 'e's got a bloke wif 'im at the moment." He sucked his teeth. "Could be you know 'im. Leastways, 'e's been asking questions about you."

"Me?"

Butterflies invaded Regina's stomach. Could it possibly be her father? "Did you hear the gentleman's name?"

"As to that, missus, maybe I did, and maybe I didn't."

Quelling a desire to throttle the lout, she said, "Was his name Farrington?"

Burt shook his head. "That's not it. Don't know this bloke's name, but 'e's been 'ere before, I can tell you that much. Just a few days ago, it was. That time, 'e give me a quid to empty me budget and tell 'im all I knew about you."

Just a few days ago. Before the trip to the gardens at Cuthbert House, perhaps?

Regina did not like the suspicion that gnawed at her brain. "Is the person with your uncle a tall gentleman of about twelve stone? Well dressed, with brown hair and eyes?"

" 'E's tall, right enough, and dressed like a London swell."

"And quite handsome?"

Burt shrugged. "I reckon 'e's the kind the females fancy."

Harcourt! But why?

Why was Joel concerning himself in her private business? It made no sense. None at all. Especially not after last night when he had made it clear by his silence that he wanted no serious entanglement with her. And without such an understanding existing between them, his active interest in her affairs was officious in the extreme.

Burt patted his coat pocket. "I got summit 'ere I was willing to sell 'im if 'e come back. Only fing is, me uncle took one look at the swell's fine clothes and threw me out of the office." His tone disgruntled, he added, "And if I know me uncle, which I do, 'e's in there as we speak telling the bloke all 'e wants to know. And pocketing a stack of the ready for 'is trouble, I'll be bound.''

Regina was aghast. "You cannot mean that Mr. Newton is selling Lord Harc—the man—information that was intended for me? Information concerning the whereabouts of my father?''

"Thom Newton 'ud sell 'is old grannie's eyes, 'e would, if 'e thought a bloke was willing to open 'is pocketbook and count out the flimsiest." Burt uttered an obscenity then sucked his teeth again. "Me luck is always out. Don't reckon the bloke'll be willing to pay for me letter now.''

"Letter!" Regina said, ever hopeful. "What letter is that?''

"Well now," Burt said, an oily smile on his face, "maybe me luck is about to change for the better. Could be as someone else is curious about me letter. That right, missus?''

Regina was furious with herself for standing in the middle of the street conversing with this common extortioner, hoping to glean crumbs of information vital to her future. Even angrier that she was at the mercy of such unprincipled men to aid her in finding her father, she yanked open the strings of her reticule and withdrew a pound note. "Here," she said, "take this, and give me the letter.''

Burt snatched the money, shoved the letter into her hand, then turned and ran.

It took only a moment for Regina to realize the letter she held was one she had written to Newton seeking his help. Unable to believe her own gullibility, she said, "But this is—'' She stopped, for argument was futile; Burt was already ducking into a dingy little grog shop.

Livid with rage, she turned and hurried toward Thom

Newton's door, ready to give him and Lord Harcourt several pieces of her mind. Unfortunately, when she burst into the musty little office, she found only one man there.

"Good day, madam," said the ferret-faced little man sitting behind one of the two battered desks. "How may I help you?"

Joel lost no time in returning to the Old Ship and ordering his curricle brought around.

"Shall I have refreshments sent up while you wait, m' lord?" the valet asked.

"No. Just apprise me the instant the carriage is ready. I shall be traveling to a little village called Pedhurst. Do you know it?"

"If I am not mistaken, there was a signpost bearing that name somewhere between here and Steyning."

"To the west, then?"

"Yes, m'lord. Probably no more than an hour's drive."

While the valet saw to the ordering of the curricle, Joel took a moment to refresh himself. He was standing before the looking glass adjusting his cravat when a knock sounded at the door.

"Harcourt. Are you there?"

"Damnation," he muttered. Curbing his impatience, he called out, "Come in, Oliver."

Needing no more than a quick glance to ascertain that his young cousin was looking decidedly down pin, he bade him be seated. "You are looking fagged, old fellow. Did my aunt never warn you of the consequences of burning the candle at both ends?"

"Perhaps," Oliver admitted, brushing his fingers through his disheveled hair. After flinging himself into the chair, he slouched way down in it, his legs akimbo, for all the world as though he had not the energy to sit up straight. "Unfortunately, my mother never warned me about duplicitous females. About wolves in sheep's clothing. Schemers. Those who practice artifice. Females who—"

"Yes, yes. I believe I have a tolerable grasp of your complaint. Perhaps you could get to the point."

Oliver moaned, then he rubbed his palms into his eyes. "*You* might have alerted me. If our situations had been reversed, I would have told you."

Joel was reasonably certain he knew what the lad had discovered. Still, it behooved him to proceed with caution; especially since duplicity was the order of the day. "If you had been in my shoes, my boy, and I in yours, what would you have told me?"

"The truth!"

"Have a care, Oliver."

There was warning enough in Joel's voice to cause the young man to sit up straight at last. "Your pardon, sir. I meant no insult. It is just that you chose to give me hints when you might have been a bit more straightforward."

"Cut line, Oliver. What lady are we discussing?"

"What lady? Felicity, of course. Can there be any doubt?"

Joel refrained from commenting upon that particular assumption.

"If only you had spoken outright, Harcourt, instead of giving me such hints as I was too stupid to understand."

"Nay, lad. You were not stupid. In my experience, when it comes to the ladies, even the best of men can be a bit shortsighted."

"Not you. You knew what Felicity was. When I called you to task for implying that I might be developing a tendre for her, I called her a little girl, but you, you observed that she was *petite.*"

"Yes," Joel said, "I believe I did say something of that nature."

"And when I referred to her as a charming child, your response was that she was a charming minx." He sighed, and the sound ended in a half sob. "She is seventeen," he said.

Joel walked over to the window to look out for his curricle. "I thought her about that age."

After taking several deep breaths, Oliver sounded more himself. "I do not scruple to inform you, cousin, that I was never more shocked. I could not believe her capable of such duplicity, and if I had not been thinking myself some curst *debauche* for having kissed her, I—"

When he stopped abruptly, Joel turned from the window. "Ah," he said quietly, "you kissed her."

Oliver's face turned redder than Joel had ever seen it before. "I . . . I never meant to kiss her. We had taken the telescope out to view the morning star, and I happened to mention that I would be returning to Dray Manor in a few days. I never dreamed she would cry. The sound of her sobs. Her tears. Harcourt, you cannot imagine what those tears did to me."

"As to that," he drawled, "I may have a fairly accurate notion."

Oliver seemed not to notice his cousin's sarcasm. "Those tears were like a hand," he said. "A giant hand that reached in and twisted my very insides. Then, without realizing what I was doing, I put my arms around Felicity to offer her comfort. It seemed the most natural thing in the world to do, and suddenly it just . . . just . . ."

"I know what it *just*, so you may spare yourself the telling of what passed between you and Miss Felicity. Depend upon it, a man does not live to be thirty-one years old without knowing all the ways a fellow can lose his head. Especially when dealing with a combination of stars and a pretty girl."

"Oh, you must not blame Felicity! In that, at least, I am persuaded she is an innocent. The fault was entirely mine."

Joel took leave to doubt that last statement, but he kept his skepticism to himself. Felicity Mitchell was a healthy, energetic young lady, and if she had been kissed, he suspected she took an active part in the episode.

"I should like to know, Oliver, what it is you wish me to say, or do, or advise."

"I need to know if I have compromised Felicity. And if so, aught I to do the honorable thing? You know, go over and make her an offer of marriage."

For the first time in years, Joel was at a loss for words. This was serious, indeed, for how could he advise a young man to do—or not do—something that would effect his entire life? It was imperative that he tread warily here.

"Putting aside your anger at the young lady's deception, Oliver, and your guilt about the kiss, how do you feel about her? Do you like her?"

"I—"

"No. Do not tell me. It is you who need to know. And while you consider that answer, there is another question you may wish to ask yourself."

"And what is that question?"

"If you were obliged to spend the next fifty years with Miss Felicity, could you imagine an affection growing between the two of you, or do you feel you would come to dislike her more and more for the deception she played?"

This time, Oliver said nothing. After a moment, he rose

from the chair and walked to the door. "Thank you, cousin.
I knew you would help me."

"Leave all to me," Thom Newton had instructed Regina.
"I will hire a gig and come round for you at The Knight's
Arms tomorrow afternoon."

Regina supposed she should be grateful to the man, for
there was no one she could ask to drive her to Pedhurst,
and since she could not handle the ribbons herself, she
would have been obliged to hire a stranger to drive her.
However, she could not overcome the feeling that she was
being manipulated. By whom, and to what purpose, she
could not say, but it was exceedingly frustrating for a
woman of intelligence and common sense to be constantly
confronted by men who felt it their right to take decisions
out of her hands.

She had wanted to go in search of her father that very
minute, but Thom Newton said he was not available until
the next day. Nor would he hand over to her Sir Nigel
Farrington's direction.

"But Gina," Constance said, once the whole had been
revealed to her, "it may be as well that you not go alone.
If Sir Nigel should prove a difficult man, Mr. Newton can
intercede for you."

"But I neither need nor want an interceder."

She began to pace the room, hoping to take the edge
off her anger. "As for Sir Nigel proving difficult, why
should he? He has been knighted. Such a man must have
a reasonable amount of good qualities, else he would not
have merited such a distinction."

"For your sake, I hope it may be so."

"Regardless of his character, or lack thereof, if I am his

daughter, he has only to accept or reject me. The choice is his.''

''And if he is not your father?''

''If that should prove to be the situation, I have but to beg his pardon for the intrusion and take myself off.''

Regina was still pacing when one of the inn porters knocked at the door, in his hand a note for Felicity. ''The gentleman is waiting belowstairs,'' he told Constance. ''If it should happen that miss is gone out, I am to take him the message. However, if she is in, he says please to inform her that he will wait twenty minutes.''

Constance and Regina exchanged questioning glances.

''My sister is in,'' Constance said. ''Be so good as to direct the gentleman to wait. And inform him that I will deliver his note.''

As soon as the porter bowed himself out, she went to the bedchamber where Felicity, still wearing her night rail and wrapper, lay upon the counterpane. When the door opened, the prostrate young lady pulled a pillow over her face.

''My dear,'' Constance said, ''I have a message for you.''

Felicity's response was muffled by the pillow. ''If you love me, go away and leave me in peace. Please.''

Her sister paid no heed to the request but approached the bed and snatched away the pillow, only to discover the usually happy pixie face was unsmiling and streaked with tears.

''The message is from Mr. Drayson,'' she said.

Immediately, Felicity sat up, dashing the tears away with the back of her hand. ''Oliver? Is he here?''

''Belowstairs. He desires you will read this note. If he has not received a response from you within twenty minutes, he means to depart.''

The young lady grabbed the missive, tore open the seal with unseemly haste, and read through the half dozen hastily scrawled lines. When she looked up again, her gray eyes were watery but hopeful. "He wants me to accompany him for a walk along the beach."

"And what of you?" Constance asked. "Is that what you want?"

She nodded vigorously. "Oh, yes. I must see Oliver. I must have an opportunity to apologize, to explain to him why I did what I did. I cannot bear to think of his going away angry with me. I have reconciled within myself that he and I will never be more than friends, but at the very least, I must have the solace of his friendship."

"Felicity! Are you telling me that you want more than friendship from Mr. Drayson? Can it be that he has engaged your affections?"

"*Engaged my affections?* Such insipid words for what has transpired. I love him, Constance. I love him with all my heart."

"Love him? But surely you are not sufficiently aquainted to—"

"If I should live to be a hundred years old, I should never love any man but Oliver."

After a moment of stunned silence, Constance turned and hurried across the room, yanked open the door to the chiffonnier, and began searching among her sister's dresses. "Where is that new yellow muslin you had from the seamstress just before we left Burwish? The one with the square neck and the double flounce at the hem."

While she searched out the frock, she bade Felicity wash her face then twist her hair atop her head. "And see you pull some curls down to rest against your neck, for I have heard it said that gentlemen find the style complimentary to the curve of a lady's throat.''

''Constance!'

''Do not argue. There is no time. You must trust my judgment in this, my dear, for I think the very least you owe Mr. Drayson is to allow him to see his *friend* in her true light.''

If Constance had been privy to the look on Mr. Drayson's face some twenty minutes later, when Felicity descended the broad staircase, she would have been granted proof of the wisdom of her sisterly advice.

''Felicity,'' the young man said, his dazed expression reminiscent of one who is unable to believe the evidence of his own eyes, ''You look beautiful.''

While the young couple stood in the foyer of the inn, not certain what they should do, Lord Harcourt tooled his curricle toward Pedhurst, assured of his mission. Driving through gently undulating hills and valleys, he soon reached the small village that lay nestled in a gap in the Downs cut by the River Arun. A quiet village, very neat and prosperous looking, Pedhurst was made up of seventeenth- and eighteenth-century half-timber cottages, the type with overhanging second stories.

Just past the tollhouse was a seventeenth-century granary made of timber and brick, and beyond that stood a black-smith's shop, fairly new, where a pair of handsome Shire horses were tied out front, awaiting the smith's attention. Deciding to stop there, Joel inquired of the large, massively built man in the leather apron if he could direct him to Wilton Manor.

''Nothing easier, sir. You'll want to follow the high street.

Once you reach the top of the village, where the church marks the end of the street, you'll see freshly painted pales, crossed over by a stile, then finally a set of wooden gates. Very white they are.'' He smiled. ''My boy painted the pales and the gates for Sir Nigel just last week.''

Joel thanked the man for his help, then he continued on his way. Within a matter of minutes he was beside the old parish church with its beautifully carved Norman arch and door. To his right, glistening in the afternoon sunlight, were the promised white pales. Turning in at the open gates of the estate, he drove up an unpretentious, though well-kept carriageway. The house was visible almost immediately.

It was a handsome Tudor manor, comfortable rather than large, and its most appealing feature was the diamond-shaped, lead-pane windows set in centuries-old stone frames. The dark oak of the heavy entrance door was continued in the wide plank floors and paneling of the vestibule, and as Joel stepped inside, the homey smell of beeswax filled his nostrils.

After presenting his card to the elderly butler and asking him to inquire if Sir Nigel would receive him, Joel was led to the hall where he seated himself upon a tall upholstered settle placed close to the flagstone hearth of a welcoming fire.

''I will inform Sir Nigel that you are here, my lord.''

In view of the pleasant atmosphere of the house and the proper, yet well-mannered, servant, Joel found it difficult to remember that he was disposed to dislike the owner of the establishment. After all, this was the man who had married and then deserted Regina. This was the man Joel had pictured himself felling with a bullet to the heart.

Expecting the butler to return, Joel was surprised to see a tall, robust gentleman of military bearing approaching him, a smile upon his face and his hand extended in welcome.

"Lord Harcourt," he said, "happy to see you. I have only just come in from visiting one of my tenants, and Bishop was to bring a pot of tea and some of Mrs. Bishop's hot cross buns to the library. I would be pleased if you would join me, sir."

Momentarily sidetracked by the man's unaffected cordiality, Joel took the proffered hand and agreed to the tea and buns. It was only after they took their places in the comfortable chairs on either side of the carved oak fireplace that Joel became aware that Farrington's once black hair was liberally sprinkled with gray, and that there were fine lines around his mouth and at the corners of his eyes.

My God! The man is fifty if he is a day.

What could have prompted Regina to marry a man twice her age—a man old enough to be her father? And why, by all that was holy, had Farrington chosen to desert her—desert the most beautiful, the most exciting woman Joel had ever met? Other than the desertion being a deplorable act, it made no sense at all for a middle-aged man to leave such a wife.

"Sir Nigel," he said, "before I impose further upon your hospitality—"

"No imposition at all, my lord. Always happy to have a visitor."

"Be that as it may, I feel it only proper for me to apprise you of my purpose for calling upon you."

"If you feel you must, sir, you may tell me anything you like, though I assure you, you are welcome no matter what your mission." He smiled then settled back against the leather cushioning of the chair, as if preparing himself for a comfortable coze. " 'Tis my years in the military, I suppose. I grew accustomed to being always in company, and now that I am retired, and living alone in this big house, I find I miss the noise and the constant bustle of activity.''

The man's openness was appealing, and Joel was obliged to remind himself that Sir Nigel Farrington was a scoundrel.

"You will be surprised, no doubt, Sir Nigel, to discover that I am acquainted with a lady who bears the same name as you. A lady who has chosen to introduce herself about Brighton as a widow.''

"Oh,'' his host replied, a questioning look upon his face. "Are you supposing, my lord, that the lady and I might be connected? Though I assure you I should be happy to discover a relative, widowed or not, I fear I am alone in the world, and have been for a quarter of a century. I know of no Farrington relations, not even distant ones.''

The blackguard! He lied with the skill of a serpent.

All Joel's previous dislike of the fellow returned. "No relatives at all?'' he asked, his tone implying that he very much doubted the assertion. "None?''

The affable look finally left Sir Nigel's face. "As I said, my lord.''

"And do you tell me as well, sir, that you know nothing of a place called Byrn Park? If your memory needs refreshing, the estate is situated near the village of Burwish, in East Sussex.''

The man swore, and the once friendly hazel eyes narrowed menacingly. "What is this about?''

"It is about the lady. The lady who calls herself Mrs. Farrington. But forgive me, you said you did not know her.

Perhaps it might help you to remember if I inform you that she was once known as Miss Anne Regina Mitchell."

Nigel Farrington all but leapt from his chair, his hands balled into fists. "Get out of here, you cur! Get out before I throttle you with my bare hands!"

Chapter Eleven

"Throttle me" Joel asked calmly, "simply because I mention Miss Anne Regina Mitchell?"

"How dare you make free with my wife's name!"

"And how dare you, sir, forget her so easily."

"Forget her?" Pain shadowed Sir Nigel's eyes. "Not a day goes by that I do not think of her. Not an hour in that day passes that I do not miss her . . . grieve for her."

Joel could not doubt the sincerity of the older man's words or the honesty of feeling in his voice. He may have deserted her, but he loved her still.

"We were married such a short time," Sir Nigel continued. "A matter of weeks, actually. Then all my happiness was taken from me."

Suddenly not at all certain that his anger against this man was deserved, Joel asked Farrington if he would tell him what had happened. "Why did you leave her?"

"I have no idea who you are, or how you came to know

so much of what is both private and painful to me. However, since you seem to know so much, Lord Harcourt, I
will assume that you are aware the lady was but seventeen
when we wed."

*Seventeen! So young. That explained how Regina had made
the mistake of marrying a man twice her age.*

"Do you know Mitchell?" Farrington asked. "Sir Hubert
Mitchell, Baronet?"

Joel shook his head. "The gentleman is deceased. I never
met him."

"Do not repine. To meet him was to dislike him. To
know him was to detest him. Mitchell was totally selfish,
and forever in debt, and he had hopes of marrying his
sister to some wealthy neighbor who had agreed to pay
Mitchell's most pressing debts."

Sir Nigel drank deeply from his cup, as though needing
the strong tea to wash away the taste of uttering Sir Hubert
Mitchell's name. "When she informed her brother of her
affection for me, he refused his consent to our betrothal
and began to bring more pressure to bear regarding the
neighbor. My poor Anne grew more anxious by the day.
He was her guardian and she was still four years from her
majority."

"Could nothing be done?"

"Only one thing. We agreed upon an elopement. As
you can imagine, neither of us would have chosen that
course if we had not been convinced her brother meant
to see her wed within a matter of days."

"So you married her."

"Yes. And for a few brief days we were happy. She loved
me, and I adored her."

Joel found he did not like to hear that Regina loved this

man, no matter what her provocation to marry. "If, as you say, you adored her, then why did you abandon her?"

"I did no such thing! Never. It would have been less painful to tear out my own heart."

Remembered anger burned deep in his eyes. "Mitchell found us. He brought a pair of armed ruffians, and they held me down while he dragged my young bride from the room."

"Where did he take her?"

Sir Nigel merely stared into his tea cup. "I know not. Suffice to say, he hid her well. I could not find her, though I searched day and night. Within a matter of weeks, I received a letter from Mitchell's man of business informing me that the marriage had been annulled on the grounds that his sister had agreed to a prior contract."

Annulled. Joel felt unbelievably cheered by the word. Could it be that Regina was not married after all?

"It was not true, of course," Sir Nigel said. "Anne had not agreed to any such contract. When I tried to visit her, Mitchell threatened to bring charges against me for a clandestine marriage. He said he would have me transported as a felon if I tried to contact his sister again."

"What happened then?"

When he answered, his tone was dull, all animation gone from his features. "Shortly after that, my regiment was sent to Canada."

"And you never saw her again?"

Sir Nigel shook his head slowly, the motion conveying the sadness of his memories. After setting his cup and saucer on the small table to his right, he rested his head against the back of the chair and closed his eyes. "The week of her twenty-first birthday, I wrote to Anne. My letter was returned, the seal unbroken, with a short note from Mitchell informing me that his sister had died.''

Died! Joel could not credit that a brother would utter such lies about his sister. The man was despicable! To ruin her life for his own ends was bad enough, but to temp fate by alleging her death was an abhorrence.

And what of Farrington? One had only to look at the man to see the depth of his sorrow. He had loved her. It mattered not that Joel had come to Pedhurst perfectly willing to do away with the man who deserted Regina. Nor was it of any consequence that Sir Nigel was much too old for her. As for his own feelings for the lady, Joel refused even to contemplate those.

Truth was truth, and there was no avoiding it. If Mitchell had lied about his sister being dead, it was every bit as likely that he had lied about the annulment. They might still be married.

"It is not true," Joel said.

Sir Nigel opened his eyes. "What is not true?"

"Regina. She is not dead."

"Regina? Forgive me, my lord, but I do not understand what you—"

"Anne," Joel corrected. "Your wife. She is called Regina now, and she is very much alive. At this very moment she is in Brighton, staying at The Knight's Arms with her cousins, Constance and Felicity Mitchell. At least, she called them her cousins. But that is neither here nor there. What matters is that she has been searching for you, sir, for several years."

Oliver Drayson put his hand beneath Felicity's elbow to assist her across the rough shingled beach. The pinkish-brown expanse was nearly deserted at this time of the afternoon, and as they walked westward, away from the bathing machines, they remarked upon the strength of the waves that threw themselves against the shore, while out on the gray waters of the Channel, sailboats appearing no bigger than a thumbnail seemed to disappear beneath the swells only to reappear again moments later unharmed.

"I have come to love the sea," Felicity said, grasping the hood of her capote when the wind threatened to lift it from her head.

"I as well," Oliver replied, holding his beaver on firmly with one hand.

The subject obviously exhausted, they strolled for some time in silence, the only sound the crashing waves and the raucous call of the ever-present birds overhead.

"Mrs. Drayson is well?"

"Yes, thank you, my mother is in excellent health."

"Her toe is mending, I trust."

"I believe it must be, for she has not remarked upon it much of late."

They continued to walk, both feigning interest in a fisherman's boat, the kind seen by the hundreds in the waters around Brighton. A wizened old fellow pulled the pointed end of the small wooden vessel onto shore, while his companion, much younger and stronger, pushed from behind at the flat end.

"Must have finished early," Oliver remarked.

"Or had trouble in the rough water," Felicity suggested.

With nothing more to offer on that topic, they fell silent once again.

Several minutes passed, and as if on cue, they both spoke at once.

"Oliver."

"Felicity."

"Excuse me," he said. "You go first."

"No, please. You go."

He cleared his throat. "Felicity I have been thinking."

"You have?"

"Yes."

"About what?"

"About you and me. About what we did earlier. You know, when we went to look at the morning star."

Pleased that he wished to discuss something she had been unable to put from her mind these eight hours and more, she stopped and looked directly at him. "You refer to the kiss."

He cleared his throat again. "Yes. The kiss. I want you to understand that I take full responsibility. It was entirely my fau—"

"Was it not wonderful?" she said. "I have never been kissed before, not by a man, I mean, but I am persuaded there was never a more exciting kiss. Do you not agree, Oliver?"

When Mr. Drayson's face turned a dark red, the young lady took that as encouragement and rushed into her explanation.

"I know you are angry with me, Oliver, and though I never meant for you to be, I am persuaded you have every right, for I did fool you into thinking I was a child, but if you would only let me explain how I came to be dressed thus, you would see it was never my intention to do more than make it easier on Gina's pocketbook, for you must know she had only the five hundred pounds, and if I was a young lady, too, it would be so much more expensive." She paused, looking up him. "You do understand, then, why I did it?"

The young gentleman blinked. "I suppose so. That is, it is not *perfectly* clear, but I believe you meant no harm."

"Oh, Oliver!" she said, throwing herself upon his chest, her arms twining around his slim waist, "I knew you must forgive me when you heard the whole."

With her soft body pressed against his, it seemed irrelevant to Oliver that he knew no more than he had ten minutes ago. Her hood had finally blown off to hang forgotten down her back, and while her forehead rested against his chin, the sweet, clean aroma of her filled his nostrils. He breathed deeply. Heaven help him, but she smelled so good.

He knew he should tell her that people might be watching them. He knew he should insist that she unhand him and move away. When he tried to form the words, however, his arms went around her instead. Vowing on his honor to do no more than allow her to hug him if that was her wish, he locked his fingers together—locked them to insure that his hands did not stray to her soft back, an idea that was tempting in the extreme.

"Oh, Oliver," she said again, nestling her face in his neck cloth in a way that caused an unusual warmth beneath the starched linen. As well, with her standing thus, one of the curls that had been whipped loose from her coiffure, a victim of the sea breeze, chanced to brush against his lips.

Back and forth the tress moved, teasing his mouth until he thought he would go mad. Finally, when he could abide the torment no longer, he pursed his lips and blew the curl away. Unfortunately, Felicity chose that very moment to look up at him, catching him in the act of blowing.

Completely misinterpreting his motives, she murmured, "Oh, Oliver," and raised herself on her tiptoes so that her mouth was mere inches from his. "Please," she said, "kiss me all you like. For it is what I want above all else."

Remembering her innocence, he tried manfully to deny himself the full pink lips so agonizingly close. Unfortunately, when she tightened her hold around his waist, it was as though her action forced his head down, for without his knowing how it came to be, his mouth was on hers.

Just as it had happened that morning, one kiss became two, then three, each blending into the other until Oliver could not imagine a worse fate than being obliged to end this sweet torment.

His fingers refused to stay locked, and he found his hands exploring the slight yet entrancing curve of her back, the delicate shoulder blades, and the soft, unbelievably smooth skin at the nape of her neck.

And still the kiss continued.

He caressed her warm nape, and the silken texture of her flesh beneath his fingertips, made even sweeter by the fact that she did not pull away from his touch, nearly drove him distracted. All that saved him from the heat that threatened to turn him to a pile of ashes was the sudden and rather dramatic intervention of a wave that came crashing onto the shore, the cold water hitting against the back of his legs and calling him to a return to sanity.

Though the effort required more resolve than he knew he possessed, he took firm hold of Felicity's shoulders, setting her away from him. "Little one," he said, the voice so hoarse he barely recognized it as his own, "we must stop."

"Why?" she asked softly.

When he looked into her upturned face, her eyes had

a sleepy quality that did something to his solar plexus, and her lips were parted and slightly swollen, forcing him to remind himself that they were on a public beach. Even if they had been the only two people for miles, he had to remember that she was far too unworldly to know how dangerous this activity could be.

"Felicity," he said, giving her a gentle shake until she opened her eyes completely. "We cannot do this here."

She mewed like a little kitten. "Then where may we do it?"

Oliver was forced to let go her shoulders and step some distance away. "Stay there!" he ordered when she moved as if to follow him. "Do not come any closer. I have had about all I can endure."

His harsh words stopped her. "But I thought you liked kissing me."

Her voice sounded as though it might break, and a suspicion of tears glistened in her eyes. Oliver took a deep breath, hoping to strengthen his resolve, for it was all he could do not to close the distance between them and take her in his arms again.

"Do not cry!" he ordered. "Under no circumstances are you allowed to cry! That is what got us into this trouble in the first instance. If you had not cried this morning, I might never have kissed you, then I would not be standing here aching to kiss you again."

When she blinked, the thick damp lashes threatened to adhere to the soft skin just beneath her eyes. Then she smiled, and that smile put him in mind of sunshine after the rain. So warm. So welcome. So utterly loveable.

"Then you liked kissing me?" she asked softly.

"Liked it? I loved it. Fact of the matter is, Felicity, I love you."

"You . . . you do?"

"Yes, but I was not aware of my true feelings until I had time to think through a question my cousin Harcourt posed earlier."

Felicity stared at him as if unable to believe what she had heard. "What did he ask?"

"He asked how I would feel if I were obliged to spend the next fifty years with you. Could I imagine an affection growing between us."

"And what was your answer?"

"I did not have one at that time."

This time she took the deep breath, as though needing to fortify herself against all possibilities.

"Do you have an answer now? Could you imagine an affection growing between us?"

"Oh, yes. Affection and more. In fact, my love, I believe I would not want to live those fifty years if I could not live them with you."

"Oh, Oliver."

"Now," he said, his knees feeling decidedly wobbly, "I have a question to put to you. Two, actually."

She stared at him expectantly, as if only waiting for him to get through asking so she could give him her answer.

"Question number one. Will you be my wife?"

"Oh, Oliver, I—"

"And question number two. Will you please stop saying, 'Oh, Oliver'?"

"Yes and yes!" she cried, then she crossed the distance between them, running into his open arms. "I will marry you."

He kissed her once again, just to seal the bargain, and

when he raised his head to look into her eyes, she said, "Oh, Oliv—"

She stopped herself just in time, then she smiled up at him in such an impish way that he was obliged to kiss her one more time.

Chapter Twelve

That evening, in the sitting room of the suite, the news of Felicity's betrothal was greeted with squeals, hugs, and a flattering degree of good wishes. Not even her sister's sudden departure to write a note to Lieutenant Seaforth could dampen the happiness of the bride-to-be.

"Oliver took me to see his mother, of course," she told Regina, "for he could not slight her in something so important as the information that we were to be wed. Aside from the fact that she is his guardian for four more months, he is quite devoted to her."

Regina nodded in agreement with his reasoning. "The attention does him credit. How did Mrs. Drayson greet the news? Did she pose any objections?"

"She was justifiably surprised," Felicity said, her smile giving way to a serious expression. "At the onset she even refused to discuss the matter. However, once Oliver informed her that we would be wed no matter what arguments were put forth to disuade us, she gave in with as much grace as could be expected.''

"Good for her," Regina said. "She made a wise decision.''

"And good for Oliver, as well," Felicity insisted. "Was he not masterful?''

Regina managed to hide her smile. "Of a certainty. On the subject of your fiancé's finer qualities, I am persuaded there can be no two opinions.''

Pleased to have her sentiments confirmed, Felicity regaled her cousin with all the most interesting particulars of her beloved's proposal and his magnanimous nature in forgiving her deception. "Though his mother was want to be a bit reproving on the subject of my disguise.''

"Tweaked your nose, did she?''

Felicity giggled. "My future mama-in-law would never be so rude. Actually, once I explained my reasons to her satisfaction, she was so gracious as to bid me come kiss her cheek.''

Regina was pleased to hear that piece of news, for she wished her young cousin all the joy in the world. Not that anyone witnessing the sparkle in Felicity's wide gray eyes could doubt her happiness.

"Has a date been decided upon for the happy event?''

"Not yet. Oliver and I are to discuss that matter this evening. Oh! I very nearly forgot to mention the invitation.''

"What invitation is that?''

"Mrs. Drayson wishes to celebrate the engagement with a small dinner party. Nothing elaborate, just something to mark the occasion.''

"A nice gesture.''

"Then you will come? Oh, Gina, how wonderful! I was

afraid you might think it awkward. Now I shall have my entire family with me. I cannot tell you how happy that makes me."

Regina had not meant to imply that she would be present at the party, but one look at her cousin's radiant face, and she could not find it in her heart to refuse.

"It is to be a small gathering, principally the two families. I believe Mrs. Drayson said she hoped to seat eight. That is, it will be eight if Lieutenant Seaforth is available."

Not for one instant did Regina question the likelihood of the military gentleman's availability. With Felicity's future assured, Regina had no doubt that Constance was at that very moment writing Seaforth, encouraging him to renew the proposal she had refused the evening before.

"You said there would be eight at the party. Were there not six before?"

"Yes, but this time you will be there, making number seven."

"And the eighth?"

Felicity shook her head. "It is some friend of Lord Harcourt's who is to visit him tomorrow. I do not believe he mentioned the name."

"Harcourt was there?"

"Yes. He arrived just as I was leaving, so we barely exchanged words. But he seemed pleased by the announcement of our coming nuptials."

At the mention of Harcourt's name, Regina experienced that familiar weight pressing upon her heart, the pressure bringing with it a sadness for what could never be. The ache was now so familiar she felt as though it had been a part of her for aeons. Could it be only last evening that she had discovered she loved Joel Harcourt?

Less than twenty-four hours had passed since he had

called her his sweet, beautiful colleen, then held her in his arms and kissed her—kissed her as though she meant as much to him as he meant to her. Twenty-four hours, yet the joy she had known at his nearness now seemed an eternity ago.

Regina had resolved to stay far away from him, and to accept no more invitations that would throw her into his company. Yet how could she disappoint her cousin on so important an occasion? She could not, of course. There was no avoiding it, she must go to the engagement party.

"You can wear your emerald satin," Felicity said. "And your domino."

"No!" The very thought of donning those clothes again—clothes she would forever associate with Joel and the love she bore him—seared a path of pain straight through to her soul.

Forcing a calm she did not feel, she said, "For all our sakes, I cannot abandon my role as chaperone. Not just yet. Until we are ready to forsake Brighton, I must maintain the ruse of the widow. To be discovered at this point would be to invite a scandal that could ruin both yours and your sister's names."

Felicity blushed. "As to the ruse, I hope you can forgive me, Gina, but I told Oliver everything."

"You told him? That I was not a widow?"

"I could do nothing else, not after I had vowed there would be no more pretense, and promised from that moment I would always be completely honest with him. A total confession of our Brighton scheme seemed as good a place as any to start."

Regina could find no fault with a policy of honesty, though she might have preferred her cousin to delay the beginning of her new lifestyle for a day or so. "Was Oliver quite disgusted with me?"

"He was surprised, though not nearly so dismayed by the information as was his mother."

"His mother! You told Mrs. Drayson that I was playing a part?"

"Oliver told her. That is why I suggested that you wear your domino. In a private party such as this, you will now have no need for your veil."

No need! There was every need. Regina had counted on the veil to shield her from Joel's far-too-observant scrutiny. One look at her and he would know she loved him. She would be unable to hide the fact. All she had was her pride, and she would no longer have that once Joel guessed what was in her heart.

"So you see," Felicity continued, "with all our secrets out in the open, we are now free to enjoy what remains of our time in Brighton."

Since Regina could not disabuse her of that optimistic notion without revealing her own broken heart, she decided to let tomorrow's worries wait for tomorrow. For now, she would let Felicity enjoy her day and her new-found love unfettered by her cousin's sadness.

It was not to be wondered at that Regina had mixed feelings not many hours later when both Constance and Felicity entertained their young men. The tea tray had come and gone, and both her cousins had found corners of the sitting room in which to enjoy quiet conversations with their respective fiancés. Regina was delighted for them, most sincerely delighted, yet there was no denying the fact that their happiness served to underscore her own heartbreak.

"Oh, Gina," Constance had said only minutes after Lieutenant Wesley Seaforth's arrival, "I am so happy. After I refused Seaforth last evening, he decided that if he must leave the military to gain my hand, he would do so. He had worked it out that he and I, along with Felicity, would live in the dower house on his brother's estate. Was that not magnanimous of him, to be willing to give up his career for me? Is that not the most romantic thing you ever heard?"

Regina agreed that it was indeed romantic.

"And only consider how happy we shall both be. Seaforth can now enjoy his career as long as he likes, and I shall be able to accompany him wherever he goes, forever warmed by the fact that he was willing to give it all up for me, and confident in the knowledge that my sister is well provided for."

Unable to contain her exuberance, Constance embraced her cousin, kissing her on both cheeks. "Is it not wonderful, Gina, how everything has turned out so perfectly?"

"Wonderful," she replied, albeit quietly.

Leaving the two sisters to chaperone one another, Regina claimed the headache and retired to her room where she need not watch her cousins and their young men in there new-found joy. Unfortunately, once in her bedchamber, she gained solitude but no solace. As she lay upon her bed, her eyes shut tight in hopes of blotting out Lord Harcourt's image, all she could see was his mouth, a mocking smile pulling at the corners.

"The headache, Regina? Too cowardly by half."

* * *

It might have afforded Regina some comfort if she had known that Lord Harcourt was enjoying an evening quite as miserable as her own. He lay upon his bed at the Old Ship and tortured himself with images of Regina as she had looked when they drove to the Cuthbert gardens, the wind blowing little wisps of ebony hair around her face.

He would not allow himself to recall how beautiful she had looked in her emerald satin, or how entrancing she had appeared in the midsummer moonlight, her green eyes filled with the wonder of their kiss, and her lips soft and pliable and . . . No. He dare not let himself recall that, or he might be tempted to murder Sir Nigel after all.

He had done the right thing. He had told Farrington that Regina was alive. He had even arranged for the man to come to Brighton the next day for the reunion with his wife.

Secure in the knowledge that he had acted honorably, Joel should have been able to sleep. Unfortunately, he was very much afraid that he wished he and Farrington might change places. Let Sir Nigel have the honor; Joel wanted Regina.

The next morning, the two brides-to-be slept late, while Regina rose early, forced down a few nervous bites of break-fast, then dressed for her carriage ride with Thom Newton. It was useless to tell herself to relax, and though it behooved her to keep an open mind regarding her true relationship with Sir Nigel Farrington, deep within she was convinced the man was none other than her father.

Of course, she had once believed in Father Christmas— a circumstance that proved how unreliable were her instincts.

Vacillating between moments of doubt and moments of total conviction, Regina paced the sitting room floor while she waited for Thom Newton. She waited, and she waited. They had set no fixed time, but she had assumed they would travel early in the day. As *early* passed into *reasonably early* and from there into *annoyingly unpunctual,* she berated herself for not pinning the man down to a specific hour.

She had just about given up on him when one of the inn porters came to the door with a message. It was from Newton.

> *Dear Madam,*
>   *I make you my apologies, but I have been detained and am unable to come today. Enclosed is the address you sought. If you have further need of my services, I am at your disposal,*
> > *Yrs. Etc*
> > *Thom Newton*

"Blast the man!"

Regina was convinced Newton was playing a game of some sort with her, but for the life of her she could not determine what it might be, or why he played it. Whatever his reasons for not keeping his word, it was too late now to hire a carriage and driver to convey her to Pedhurst. Even if she were on the road that very minute, she might not have sufficient time to return before Felicity's party.

Though angered and discouraged at this turn of events, Regina would not disappoint her cousin, so she was obliged to delay her journey of discovery one more day. After all, her logical side told her, if meeting her father had waited

twenty-six years, it could wait another twenty-four hours.
If Sir Nigel was indeed her long-lost parent, he would be
no less so for another day's wait. And if he was not her
father, a later day would make no difference.

By early afternoon, Constance and Felicity were bustling
about the suite, preparing for the evening at Mrs. Drayson's
and chattering like a pair of sea birds. When they began
to sigh dreamily and call one another's attention to those
sterling qualities in their respective fiancés as might have
escaped the notice of an undiscerning sister, Regina determined it was time to quit the suite. Grabbing up her widow's hat, she tied the strings securely beneath her chin,
arranged the veil around her face, and took herself off for
a breath of fresh air and a bit of quiet.

Because the fashionable hour for promenading had
come and gone, the ladies and gentlemen who visited
Brighton only to see and be seen had returned to their
rented homes or lodgings, eager to prepare for whatever
entertainments the evening offered them.

Walking westward along the cliff between the town and
the sea, Regina saw no one save a few invalids seated on
benches down at the water's edge, their purpose in being
there to inhale the healthy air. In need of exercise, she
continued her brisk pace, and though the old battery had
not been a conscious destination, somehow she found herself at that exact spot along the parapet where she and
Joel had stood two nights ago to watch the fireworks display.

She paused, telling herself that it was the sight of the
white-capped waves that called to her. Or perhaps it was
the lure of the dozens of birds that soared upon the air,
occasionally diving toward the gray waters when a likely

fish ventured too close to the surface. Either of those things was enough to draw a person to the parapet; in this instance, however, Regina knew better. She had been seduced by the hope that if she stood quite still, her eyes shut, she might imagine Joel behind her as he had been on Midsummer's Night, his strong arms wound around her waist and his broad chest at her back.

While she stood thus, the breeze from the Channel lifted her veil so that it floated upon the air like giant, black butterflies, their graceful wings billowing slowly around her. Not bothering to subdue the silk, she breathed deeply of the briny air, and as it filled her lungs, she became aware of someone quite close by.

"Regina?" said a deep, masculine voice. "Is that you?"

She did not need to turn to discover who had spoken, for she would recognize that voice if surrounded by a throng of gentlemen, all calling her name.

"I saw you from a distance," Joel said quietly. "You appeared lost in thought."

"Yes," she said, not yet looking at him. "I have much to contemplate."

"Of course," he said quietly, "you will be wishing me any place but here. Forgive the intrusion."

Realizing that he meant to leave her, Regina turned quickly and caught his sleeve. "Stay," she said.

He said nothing, merely stepped beside her, looking out over the channel. When he leaned forward, resting his elbows upon the waist-high wall, Regina was able to observe him without being observed. Surely it was an illusion, but he seemed to grow more handsome each time she saw him.

A manilla brown coat stretched snugly across his hunched shoulders, the lighter shade emphasizing the tobacco brown hair that showed at his neck beneath the beaver hat. He was in profile, and his tanned face seemed more angular than usual, his chin far more stubborn.

Not daring to spare even a moment for the contemplation of his unsmiling mouth, Regina gave her attention to his coat sleeve, letting her gaze travel down the firm arms beneath the material. Her scrutiny ended at his hands. He had chosen to remove his kid gloves, placing them on the parapet, and his long, supple fingers were steepled, the pads of his fingertips moving slowly back and forth, one hand against the other.

The sight of his thick wrists, with just a hint of dark hair showing beneath the coat cuffs, had caused enough difficulty for Regina, all but stealing the breath from her lungs. But the slow, gentle motion of his fingertips was far worse; mesmerized, she feared her heart had stopped beating.

She was obliged to say something—anything—to divert her traitorous thoughts from his hands. "You are not displeased, I hope, by the engagements?"

"In the plural?" he asked, looking at her over his shoulder.

She nodded. "You are aware of the understanding between Felicity and Mr. Drayson, of course, but perhaps you had not heard that Lieutenant Seaforth made Constance an offer?"

"That is news indeed."

"It seems I am to lose both my companions almost immediately." She sighed. "I have enjoyed being back in their company this past month, and I fear I shall miss them when I am alone again."

"Alone?"

He stared at her, the look so searching Regina could not even guess what occupied his thoughts.

"Are you so certain that will be your fate?"

"Life is never certain," she said. "And Fate, if you recall your mythology, is a capricious creature."

He smiled then, though the look in his eyes was more resigned than happy. "Semantics again, madam? I believe we have come full circle in our acquaintance."

"If we are to speak of semantics, sir, allow me to remind you that a circle is a closed plane curve, seemingly without beginning or end."

"And your point, Regina?"

"I am scheduled to remain at The Knight's Arms until Saturday, at which time I shall remove to some other location. Ergo, my time at Brighton will come to an end, as will the acquaintances I have made here."

Regina had attempted to make the words light and teasing, but they had been difficult to say. She did not want to think of her acquaintance with Joel coming to an end. Loving him as she did, how was she to live in the world knowing that he, too, was in it, but that they would never meet again.

He straightened then and turned to look at her. "Permit me," he said, catching the floating veil and folding it back to reveal her face.

Regina remained perfectly still—not breathing, not even batting an eye—allowing Joel to do whatever he wished, helpless to do more herself than gaze up at him.

"There," he said, stepping back, "that is much better."

Apparently satisfied, he rested his hips against the parapet, then he reached out and took Regina's hands in his. "The other night," he said, "did I tell you how beautiful you are?"

He had, of course, and Regina had tucked those magical words away in her heart, hoping they might offer her some comfort in the years ahead.

"If I did not," he continued, giving her hands a gentle tug, urging her an inch closer, "allow me to tell you of your eyes, for they are magnificent."

"They are?"

"They are. And your skin," he said, the words almost a whisper, "is as soft as velvet and begging to be touched."

Regina knew she should pull her hands away, but in truth it was all she could do not to insinuate herself into his arms. Heaven help her, even knowing that he did not love her, she wanted him to hold her as he had during the fireworks.

"My sweet," he murmured, looking at her hands in his, "there is something else I would tell you. Something I must say now, while we are alone, for who can know when we might have another private moment together."

A private moment!

Regina's heart began to pound inside her chest. Was she imagining this, or was it truly happening? Unless she was mistaken, Joel was about to make her a declaration. For what other reason would he require a private moment?

"Yes," she said, the word so breathless it was little more than a sigh.

"You cannot doubt the degree of my admiration for you," Joel said. "I think you the finest, the most genuine lady I have even known. And," he added, his voice just a bit husky, "you are a true delight."

The huskiness of his voice did something to Regina's bones, for they seemed almost to liquify within her body. She wished he would let go of her hands so that she might touch his face. His dear, wonderful face.

"After tonight," he said, "our lives will never be the same."

Regina thought surely she would burst from happiness. He must mean to announce their engagement tonight along with the announcements of her cousins. She could not prevent the smile that pulled at the corners of her mouth. "How mysterious you are," she said, a teasing note in her voice. "Is there something special about tonight?"

He did not return her smile. "I hope with all my heart that it will prove to be so for you. You deserve nothing less. I pray that tonight will be the beginning of a lifetime of happiness for you."

She could not take much more of this sweet agony. "But what of yourself, Joel? Does the evening not hold a similar promise for you?"

"For me," he said, "it will be infinitely sad, for after tonight I shall probably never see you again."

"What! Never see me again?" Dazed, Regina pulled her hands away. "I do not understand. What are you saying?"

"What I wished you to know," he said, "what I could not leave Brighton without telling you, is that I shall never forget you. And if you ever have need of me—no matter the reason—I am yours to command. I want you to remember that I will always be your friend."

Chapter Thirteen

I will always be your friend.

Regina could not remember those words without experiencing again the embarrassment she had felt this afternoon at the parapet. How could she have been such a fool? Only a complete ninnyhammer would have heard Joel's words and twisted them so they sounded like a proposal of marriage.

"I shall never forget you," he had said.

Regina could not recall walking back to The Knight's Arms. After Joel's offer of friendship, the next few minutes were a complete blur in her mind. She must have said something to him, yet she had no idea what it might be.

All she knew was that somehow she had arrived at the entrance to the inn. Remembering to pull her veil over her face to hide the tears that coursed down her cheeks, she had entered the cobble-fronted building and climbed the wide stairs, for all the world as though her heart were not shattered into a million pieces. The remainder of the afternoon had been spent in her bedchamber adding to her heartache and embarrassment by reliving Joel's words.

Now there was Mrs. Drayson's dinner party to be got through, and neither Felicity's continued pleading, nor the calm request made by Constance, had been sufficient to dissuade Regina from wearing her widow's attire to the house on the Royal Crescent. Without the silk veil to conceal her wretched state, she knew there was no way on earth she would survive the evening.

Mrs. Beatrix Drayson pushed aside the little needlepoint footstool upon which she had propped her bound foot. "But surely, Miss Farrington, you will travel to Dray Manor for the nuptials. You will not wish to miss your cousin's wedding."

A hush fell over the first floor drawing room. Constance and Lieutenant Seaforth turned from the window where they were enjoying a private conversation, and Felicity and Oliver looked up from the book on meteors they were perusing at a loo table on the far side of the room.

"Gina!" Felicity cried. "You cannot mean what you say."

"Of course she does not," the young lady's future mama-in-law assured her. "I am persuaded Miss Farrington is just feeling a bit shy."

She reached over and patted Regina's hand. "You need have no fear, for I assure you that you will be most comfortable at Dray Manor. As for the neighborhood, you will find much to amuse you in Chiveley. Our home is situated two miles east of the village, while Harcourt Hall, my nephew's estate, is no more than three miles to the west. So you see, my dear, you shall be among friends."

Friends! The word was anathema to Regina, and she prayed never to hear it spoken again as long as she lived.

Furthermore, she could not go to Chiveley. Being in company with Lord Harcourt would be torment—a useless suffering, especially when nothing could come of it but further heartbreak. If Joel did not love her now, after holding her in his arms and kissing her with such passion, seeing her at Felicity's wedding would not alter his feelings. Much better for Regina's peace of mind if she made a clean break here in Brighton and had done with it.

"I thank you, Mrs. Drayson, but my mind is made up. I shall not come to the wedding."

It was obvious from the determination on Felicity's face that she was only waiting for Mrs. Drayson to surrender her place beside Regina on the rose brocade couch before beginning her own barrage of objections to her cousin's announcement. Detecting the light of battle in the girl's eyes, Regina excused herself and fled to the small bed-chamber their hostess had set aside for the ladies of the party.

Discovering a key in the door, Regina turned it to insure her privacy, then she snatched off her veil and tossed it upon the mahogany sleigh bed, seating herself on a small upholstered bench set in the embrasure of the window. She did not cry; after all the weeping she had done, her tears were depleted. Instead, she merely gazed out the window, observing the fiery reflection of the westering sun upon the waters of the channel, yet seeing none of the magnificence of the red and orange and gold.

After a few moments her solitude was broken, for Felicity knocked at the bedchamber door begging for admittance. "Gina," she called softly, "please let me in."

When she received no answer, the young lady knocked

again. "I do not understand why you said you would not attend my wedding, Gina, but I know it has nothing to do with your love for me or your regard for Oliver. Since you have a fondness for both the bride and the groom, your reservations must have something to do with the ceremony being held at Dray Manor."

"Go away, Felicity. Please."

"I am aware," the young lady continued, "that it will cause comment among a few high sticklers that I am not to be married from my own parish church. However, I must say I did not expect objections from you on that score, Gina."

Regina did not bother to disabuse her cousin of her assumption that the location of the wedding prevented her from attending, for how could she explain about her need to avoid being in company with Lord Harcourt.

After one or two more attempts to gain entrance, Felicity went away.

When next a knock sounded, its originator was Mrs. Drayson. "Miss Farrington," she said, "I beg you will open the door. My nephew has arrived, and he bids me ask you if you will join him in the book room. The matter, he says, is of some importance."

Regina walked over and unlocked the door, though she told herself as she did so that it had nothing to do with Joel's message. Nothing at all. It was simply because good manners would not allow her to ignore a request made by her hostess.

"Your pardon, ma'am. I wish you had not been required to seek me. Is your toe any worse for the errand?"

"Think nothing of it," the lady said, staring at Regina. This being the first time Mrs. Drayson had seen her without the veil, she said, "My dear, what a handsome woman you are to be sure."

"You are very kind, ma'am."

"Nothing of the sort, I assure you. Why, with your looks, if you but come to Chiveley, I vow I shall find you a husband within a fortnight. There is Mr. Conklin, a widower not much older than my nephew, and—" She stopped abruptly, studying Regina as though she had made an important discovery.

The warmth that had invaded Regina's cheeks at the mention of Harcourt now turned to scorching heat.

"So, my dear, that is the way the wind blows. You have formed a *tendre* for my nephew."

When Regina attempted to refute any interest in Lord Harcourt, her hostess waved the denial away. "I shall not pry into what is none of my business, Miss Farrington, for you are a woman full grown, and you must be allowed to know your own mind."

"Thank you, ma'am."

"Shall I tell Harcourt that you will meet him in the book room?"

"I would prefer not to do so."

"You need not worry that the proprieties will be offended, my dear, for he is not alone. Though, I own it is most peculiar to bring a guest to a dinner party then whisk him into a private room before introducing him to his hostess. I declare, this is turning into a most unusual evening."

Deciding that she had put her hostess to a great deal of trouble already, Regina gave in and said she would see Joel. So it was that five minutes later she made her way to the ground floor and knocked at the book room door.

"Enter," Lord Harcourt called.

Regina opened the door and stepped inside the richly paneled chamber. Because the windows faced west, the drapes had already been drawn against the coming night and the candles were lit. Joel stood beside an ornate oak desk, and in the shadows a middle-aged gentleman sat in a leather wing chair. The stranger rose at her entrance.

Joel watched Regina, his heart in his throat. She wore her widow's black, but for some reason she had chosen to dispense with the veil. Not certain how he should proceed, he lifted a candelabra from the desk top and took it to the fireplace, setting it on the mantel so that it shed a pool of light upon the tall, distinguished-looking gentleman with the salt-and-pepper hair.

Joel waited for her reaction.

"Good evening," she said quietly, curtsying in the gentleman's direction.

"Regina," Joel said, his voice sounding strained to his own ears, "you are come at last. We—"

"Regina?" repeated the gentleman, looking from the lady back to Joel. "What kind of cruel jest is this, my lord?"

"I beg your pardon?"

"Who is this woman?"

Joel thought perhaps he had not heard correctly. "This is Regina Farrington."

The gentleman's eyes filled with fury, and his mouth pulled into a tight angry line. "Regina Farrington she may be, though I take leave to doubt it, but this woman is not my wife!"

While Joel tried to digest what Sir Nigel had said, Regina moved closer, peering at the man as if not certain who he might be.

"Sir Nigel," he said, "perhaps you should look more closely."

"Do not be absurd, my lord. Do you think I would not know my own wife?"

"Of course you would, sir, I just—"

"That woman is tall and dark haired," he said. "My Anne was dainty, and fair as an angel. With eyes as blue as a summer sky."

Joel looked at Regina. She stood completely still, her hands by her side. Unnaturally silent, she stared at Sir Nigel as if trying to come to some kind of momentous decision. The air seemed charged with an emotion Joel could not identify.

As Regina drew in a ragged breath, tears filled her eyes, then they spilled over and slid slowly down her cheeks.

"Papa?" she said, the word a mere whisper.

Sir Nigel seemed taken aback, though not quite so angry as before. "I fear there has been some mistake, young lady. My wife died many years ago, and to my infinite regret, I have no children."

Regina could barely speak. The tears were falling in earnest now, but she paid them no heed. She could not take her gaze from the man before her.

"Sir," she said, "you may be unaware of the existence of a child, but I think perhaps you do have one. A daughter."

The man merely shook his head.

Not in the least disheartened by his response, Regina said, "My mother's name was Anne Regina Mitchell, and she eloped at the age of seventeen. Her brother, sir Hubert Mitchell, attempted to have the marriage annulled so his sister might marry a wealthy land owner, but when it was discovered that Mother was enceinte, the marriage was allowed to stand."

Sir Nigel grasped the chair, while a sort of animal sound escaped his throat.

"Some time before my birth, Uncle Hubert told my mother that her husband had been killed in Canada. She did not believe him, however. She insisted she would have felt it in her heart if the man she loved was no longer alive."

"Anne. Oh, my sweet Anne."

"Mother never gave up hope that one day you would return. Every day for twenty years she spoke of you, telling me how honorable you were and how brave, not letting me forget for a moment that I had a father to be proud of. Her dying wish was that I never stop looking for you. And now," Regina said, brushing away the tears, "I have found you at last."

Sir Nigel availed himself of his handkerchief, using it to dry his own face. "My child," he said. "My dear, dear child."

"Papa!" she said, running into his open arms.

Chapter Fourteen

"I am persuaded he meant it for the best," Sir Nigel said.

Father and daughter were alone in the book room, their chairs pulled up to the fireplace so they might be comfortable. Though they had been together for more than an hour, Sir Nigel still held Regina's hand, almost as if afraid to let it go.

"When Lord Harcourt explained to me that he was acting in your interest, I could not doubt his sincerity. Though I hoped against all the evidence of my senses that he spoke the truth, and that my wife was not dead as I had been told, something inside me would not let me believe fully."

"You must have been overwhelmed."

"Without a doubt, my dear. As you may imagine, I felt the need of some time to sort out my thoughts. That is why I would not come straight back to Brighton with Lord

Harcourt as he wished, but delayed my visit until this evening."

"Which is probably why," she said, "I found my journey
to Pedhurst sabotaged at every turn."

Sir Nigel chuckled. "His lordship is a very determined
man, and his 'sabotage' as you call it, was meant for your
protection. But be that as it may, at this moment I cannot
find it in my heart to censure his behavior."

He gazed at Regina as though memorizing her features.
"After all, I am here, and I have the most precious gift
anyone has ever given me. I have a beautiful daughter,
and I feel almost as though I have regained a piece of my
beloved Anne as well."

"You must meet Constance, Papa. I believe she has much
the look of my mother. I, on the other hand, am very like
my father. Or so Mother always told me. She called me
her Irish colleen, saying I had my black hair and green
eyes from the Farringtons."

Their conversation was interrupted in time by the arrival
of the butler, who related to Regina Mrs. Drayson's request
that she and her father join the family in the drawing room
for a champagne toast. "I have taken the liberty of having
a tray of sandwiches conveyed there as well, miss."

"Champagne?" Regina repeated. Recalling the purpose
for this evening's party, she rose quickly from the chair.
"I cannot believe that I forgot about Felicity's engagement.
Please, Papa," she said, holding her hands out to him,
"will you come with me? I should like to make you known
to your nieces."

"But I insist," Sir Nigel said, once the toasts had been
made to both the brides-to-be and their future grooms,

"that Constance and Felicity return with my daughter and me to Wilton Manor. Their bride clothes can be made there. We have an excellent seamstress at Pedhurst, and it will be my pleasure as their relative to stand the nonsense."

"You are very generous," Mrs. Drayson said, her foot once again upon the needlepoint footstool.

"He is kindness itself," Constance agreed. "Just the type of gentleman worthy of my Aunt Anne."

"Just so," Felicity said, rushing to the couch and planting a kiss upon the gentleman's cheek.

Joel watched this exchange from a corner chair on the far side of his aunt's drawing room. His choice of seats was deliberate, for he felt the need to put some distance between himself and the happy gathering. The evening had not gone at all the way he had expected, and mentally he still reeled from the revelations, much as one might stagger physically from a well-placed fist to the solar plexus.

The most startling fact, of course, was that Regina was not married—never had been—and that the man she sought was not her husband but her father. This changed everything. Joel's entire thought processes wanted adjusting.

"You need not hire a carriage," his Aunt Beatrix informed Sir Nigel, "for I shall be happy to take the young ladies up in my barouche as far as Pedhurst. Oliver will not mind giving up his place. He may accompany you in your whiskey, or he may ride with Lord Harcourt in the curricle."

Harcourt? Curricle? Regina had been caught up in her joyous reunion with her father and the pleasure she could see upon his face at having found a family he did not know he had, but suddenly Mrs. Drayson's words penetrated her brain. Joel was to follow them to Wilton Manor! And

Pedhurst was but twenty miles from Chiveley. She would be unable to escape being in his company; perhaps for the rest of her life.

How was such proximity to be borne? As for attending the wedding, Regina could not escape it now. She would be expected to be there. As well, she would be expected to smile and share in her cousin's happiness when all the time her own heart was breaking.

Chancing a glance to the far side of the room, Regina observed Joel sitting in a corner chair, his long legs stretched out in front of him as though he had not a care in the world. His eyelids were lowered, almost as if he slept.

It must be relaxing to be Lord Harcourt. Certainly it would be restful to remain, as he had, whole of heart. How comforting not to ache to be in the arms of the person one loved. How peaceful not to be forever imagining the sweet insistence of another's lips upon one's own. How nice to be Joel Harcourt and not be longing to spend forever in the company of just one person.

Joel knew Regina was watching him. He could feel her gaze almost as if she had reached out and touched him. So attuned was he to her every word, her every gesture, her every breath, that had they been the only two people in the room he could not have been more aware of her presence.

All his senses were on the alert. Even at a distance, he fancied he could smell that clean, womanly fragrance that was so much a part of her. His fingertips grew warm from the remembered feel of her satiny skin. His pulse throbbed imagining his mouth on hers once again, tasting the sweetness of her kiss, holding her soft pliant body close to his.

Regina felt warm all over. She continued to look at Joel, all the time wondering what it was about this man that made her respond to the sight of him. He was not even aware that she was in the room, yet her heart was racing as though he were holding her close; as though he were kissing her, his lips teasing hers, drawing from her very soul the—

"Regina," Sir Nigel said, effectively ending her fantasy, "your face is flushed. Are you quite well, my dear?"

"She is exhausted," Mrs. Drayson said, "and who can wonder at it. Such an evening as she has had. Such excitement. Such joy. I daresay the poor child is longing for the quiet of her bedchamber where she may gather her thoughts and make what she will of her disordered emotions."

Regina licked her suddenly dry lips, grateful that the lady did not know the real cause for her flushed countenance. While she tried to think of some remark that would not betray what had truly disordered her emotions, Sir Nigel rose from the couch and extended his hand to his daughter.

"Come, my child. Allow me to see you to the inn. This will be your last night spent there, for tomorrow you will take your rightful place in my home. No," he corrected, "in our home."

After donning her bonnet and veil, Regina allowed her father to see her safely to the door of her suite, but as soon as he had kissed her cheek, wished her a restful night, then departed for his own room at the Castle Inn, she tiptoed back down the wide staircase and slipped past the lone porter who nodded in his chair near the entrance. She did not wish to be present while Oliver and Seaforth bid her cousins goodnight, and she desperately wanted to feel a breath of cool air upon her face.

Once outside again, Regina looked to both right and left to make certain she was not being watched, then she hurried across the street. Staying in the shadows, she made her way to the parapet and that spot she was beginning to think of as belonging exclusively to her and Joel.

She leaned against the rough stone of the wall, gazing at the moonlit water below. The sea birds had sought their nests for the night, and all was quiet save for the pounding of the waves upon the shingled beach. The wind lifted Regina's veil as it had that afternoon, and she folded it back so the briny smell of the sea might fill her nostrils.

She had thought she was alone. In fact, she did not even see the man until he stepped out of the shadows and spoke her name, startling her and causing her to gasp in alarm.

"Regina," he said, his voice sounding strained, almost angry, "what are you doing here? Has something happened that you risk coming out alone?"

She waited until Joel was beside her before she answered. "I wanted to say goodbye to Brighton."

"You should have done better to wait for the morning. Did you think your widow's habit would protect you from those villains who seek the cover of darkness? I promise you it would not. You might have been injured."

She chose not to reply, for *he* was the only person concealed in the shadows. If the truth be known, the only hurt she had suffered while in Brighton was to her heart, and Joel Harcourt had been the unwitting perpetrator of that injury by not returning her love.

But she did not speak of that truth aloud. She could not. Instead, she changed the subject by thanking him for bringing her father to Brighton.

"You are welcome," he said. "I am happy that everything turned out so well. More happy than you know."

"I still do not understand, my lord, why you interested yourself in something that had nothing to do with you. However, I suppose it would be ungrateful of me to find fault with a course of action that ended so fortuitously."

"Yes," he agreed, "shamefully ungrateful. Especially if you had even a glimmer of a notion of the agonies I suffered when I believed you were Sir Nigel's wife."

Agonies? What was this? Did Joel mean to imply that he was—

No, no! Regina had already trod that path to self-deception earlier in the day. She would not be led down it again.

When she said nothing, Joel approached the parapet and rested his elbows on the wall, then he leaned his weight on his forearms, relaxing as though he had not a care in the world, and gazing at the moon reflected on the water. His calm demeanor convinced Regina that she had been correct in dismissing his use of the word *agonies*. Apparently he had not been serious.

When he continued to stare out at the water, Regina did likewise, placing both her hands, once again, upon the rough stone wall. For a time neither of them spoke.

"I had not expected to see you again tonight," he said.

"Nor I you."

"But perhaps our meeting was meant to be, for I have something of importance to say to you. At least," he corrected, "*I* think it important."

Regina closed her eyes, willing herself to remain calm. Forewarned, she was now forearmed, and she knew not to give Joel's words a meaning he did not intend them to have. Semantics, she reminded herself.

"You forget," she said, "that we spoke this afternoon. You told me then that you would never forget me. You were so magnanimous as to suggest that if I ever had need of you—no matter the reason—that you were mine to command." Regina found it difficult to swallow. "Then you bade me remember that you would always be my friend."

"Damnation, Regina! Do not throw my words back in my face. If you had any idea how difficult they were for me to say, you would not oblige me to listen to them being repeated."

"I will not be cursed at!" she said. "And if we are to discuss how difficult those words are for you to hear, allow me to inform you that they were no less welcome to my ears this afternoon. It may interest you to know, my lord, that I was so foolish as to think that you meant to—"

Regina stopped abruptly, appalled that she had very nearly confessed that she had thought him about to propose marriage. While she took a deep breath, hoping to still her rapidly beating heart, she felt Joel turn so that he faced her, his weight now on only his right elbow. When she stole a glance at him, he was smiling, his strong, even teeth appearing very white in the semi-darkness.

"You had thought I meant to do what?" he asked, his voice no longer serious, but light, almost teasing.

Resting as he was against the parapet, their faces were on the same level, and Regina knew that she need only lean toward him an inch or so for their mouths to be close enough to kiss. Yet she warned herself to be wary of such thoughts. Had she not very nearly made a fool of herself in this same place a few hours ago?

This time she would take nothing for granted. This time she would jump to no conclusions.

"Do you remember," he asked softly, "what I said to you before I declared myself your ever friend?"

She did, of course. How could she not remember, for he had said she was beautiful. Not certain she could hear such words again without bursting into tears, she bade him let the past remain in the past. "After all," she said, "a new life is just beginning for my cousins and me.

"The three of us came to Brighton hoping to achieve but two goals: to see Constance well married so that hers and Felicity's futures might be assured, and to try to see if I could find my father."

"And you succeeded in both instances," he said.

"As you say. Actually, we succeeded beyond our wildest dreams, for Constance will marry for love, Felicity has found the one gentleman in the world most suited to her, and I have met my father and will soon make my home with him."

"Is that to be your future, Regina? Have you no thoughts for your own happiness? Are your cousins to be the only ones to find love?"

Regina merely shook her head, for she felt suddenly breathless, as though she had run a long distance. At that moment she could not have spoken if her life depended upon it.

Joel seemed to suffer from no such affliction. When he spoke again, his voice was a soft, caressing whisper. "What of your heart, sweet Regina?"

She could not believe that he was tormenting her in this manner. Surely he must know that such particular questions would give rise to speculation in any female.

"Would you like to marry?" he asked.

Would this torment never end?

Regina wanted to scream, and she might have done so

if a very large lump had not risen to obstruct her vocal cords, making a noise of any kind virtually impossible.

Joel reached out his hand then, and with the back of his fingers he began to stroke her cheek, just in front of her ear. "Would you like to marry me?" he asked softly.

His fingers were so warm against her skin, so mesmerizing that Regina could not be certain she had not imagined his last question. "What did you say?"

As if to leave no doubt in her mind as to his intentions, Joel straightened from the parapet and caught her around the waist, pulling her hard against his chest. "I love you, my beautiful colleen, and I ask nothing more of life than to spend all my days and all my nights with you. "

With him holding her so close, Regina could feel the quickened pace of his heart, and the beat was every bit as strong and as wild as her own.

"Will you marry me?" he asked again.

Regina felt the tears well in her eyes, but this time they were tears of such exquisite happiness that she welcomed their moisture as they coursed down her cheeks.

"Here now," Joel said, gently brushing the moisture away with his finger, "none of that."

He bent to kiss her, but just before his lips touched hers, he stopped and straightened. "And no more of this blasted veil," he said, releasing her so that his hands were free to untie the strings of her bonnet.

Making quick work of the bow that secured the satin ribbons, Joel removed the offending garment. With a smile, he drew his arm across his chest, then using a sweeping backhand motion, he straightened his arm and sent the bonnet sailing beyond the parapet. "Goodbye forever," he said.

As he and Regina watched, the wind caught the detested

item and carried it aloft for several moments, the circular silk of the veil billowing out like a giant black bird on the wing.

What became of the bonnet and veil, they neither knew nor cared, for Joel had returned his attention to Regina and was holding her face gently between his hands. His gaze held hers as the breeze whipped ebony tendrils about her temples. "And now, my sweet, I am still waiting for the answer to my question."

All the longing Regina had been obliged to keep secret seemed to burst from her heart. "Yes," she said. "Yes. Yes. Yes. Yes. Yes."

The light that shown in Joel's eyes very nearly stole Regina's breath away. "Are you saying you love me" he asked, "as I love you?"

"Yes," she said again. "I love you, Joel Harcourt, with my whole heart."

"Then shall I apply to your father for your hand?"

She nodded. "But please," she said, "let's not talk anymore."

Not at all averse to this suggestion, Joel lowered his mouth to hers, kissing her with a tenderness Regina had not known existed.

"My love," he murmured against her lips. "My sweet, beautiful colleen."

While Joel traced the contours of her face with his fingertips, Regina wrapped her arms around his waist and insinuated her body as close as possible to his, offering up her lips for his kiss. He was more than happy to oblige her, and as the kiss continued, Regina thought life could offer her no more happiness than this, for she was with the man she loved, and he tasted so good, and his body felt so wonderful and strong against hers.

She changed her mind regarding the boundaries of her happiness when Joel, having given her an opportunity to lead the way, took control of the embrace. Catching her in his arms, he very nearly lifted her off her feet as he crushed her to his chest. His mouth covered hers, and as the kiss deepened, Regina realized that real happiness had no limitations.

When at last Joel tore his lips from hers and put her away, he suggested that they return her immediately to her suite at The Knight's Arms. "For I am a mere mortal, my love, and not at all certain how much of this sweet torment I can withstand."

Regina sighed, happy to know that he was as affected by her kisses as she was by his.

"Furthermore," he continued, "if you do not agree to marry me with all haste, my entrancing Regina, I cannot answer for the consequences."

Secure in her knowledge that the man she adored loved her every bit as much as she loved him, Regina reached up and ran her finger along the edge of Joel's determined chin. "I remember once, my lord, when you said you did not kiss wives."

Joel caught her finger and used it to tap playfully at the tip of her nose. "Either you are a very saucy minx, my love, or this is semantics run amok, for I distinctly remembering saying that I did not kiss *other men's* wives."

"Oh," she said, a twinkle of mischief in her eyes, "then what of your own wife?"

"My own wife?" he said, gathering Regina in his arms once again. "Now that will be a different matter altogether."

EPILOGUE

August first was a balmy, sunny day—perfect weather for a wedding—and as Regina gazed out the diamond-shaped, lead-pane window of her second-floor bedchamber, she saw her father's coachman stop the barouche before the entrance to the manor house. Pulled by four perfectly matched white horses, the carriage had been festooned with white satin ribbons.

"An equipage fit for a bride," her father had said.

Her father. After four weeks here at Wilton Manor, Regina still could not believe she had found her father, and that he had brought her to his home. No, her home. At least for another hour.

A knock sounded at her door, but before she could grant permission to enter, Felicity burst in, looking pretty as a picture in a plain white satin dress, the high waist adorned with a blue satin sash.

"It is time," she said, excitement lighting up her pixie

face, "and Uncle Nigel says if we are not downstairs within the next two minutes, he means to call the entire wedding off and keep the three of us here as old maids forever."

"The old tease," Constance said, following her sister into the room. "I declare, if any but my handsome Seaforth waited for me at the church, I might be tempted to stay here with my uncle."

Always beautiful, Constance was breathtaking in pale, sky blue silk with a white lace overdress.

"Papa has a gift for each of us," Regina said, pointing to three small boxes wrapped in silver paper.

"More gifts?" Constance exclaimed. "He is too good. Only consider the cost of three sets of bride's clothes."

"Papa enjoyed giving them to us."

"Of course he did," Felicity agreed, reaching for her gift and tearing open the paper. Inside was a velvet jeweler's box containing a diamond brooch in the shape of a star. After a suitable number of moments to let her breathing return to normal, she handed the brooch to her sister and bid her fasten it at the front of the crown of ribbons that held her lace-edged veil.

Constance attached the brooch, then she opened her own gift. Inside was a spray of sapphires the exact shade of her eyes. After pinning the jewelry at the neck of her overdress, she straightened her long silk veil so it fell in graceful folds down her back.

Regina was the last to open her gift. Her brooch was fashioned of pure, unadorned gold, and it consisted of three simple, interlocked circles. Engraved on the back of each circle was a name. Nigel. Anne. Regina. A family at last, the three of them were joined forever.

Dashing away the tears that threatened to spill down her cheeks, Regina pinned her brooch at the waist of her simple white sarcenet frock. Vowing never again to don a veil, she had chosen to wear white rosebuds threaded through her dark hair.

Glancing one last time in the looking glass above her dressing table, she saw her own reflection as well as those of her two cousins. For a moment, no one spoke, then all three young ladies smiled.

"Are you happy?" Regina asked.

"Oh, yes," Constance replied. "And you?"

"My heart is full. With such a man as my Joel, who would not be happy?"

They both looked at Felicity. "I am practically floating among the stars."

Of one accord the three brides turned and exited the room, hurrying toward the staircase where Sir Nigel waited to escort them to the church and their waiting bridegrooms.

"By the way, Gina," Felicity said, linking arms with her sister and her cousin, "you have not yet admitted that I was correct when I told you that going to Brighton was the answer to all our problems."

"Then let me admit it now," Regina said, looking down at the irrepressible girl, "you were right."

As she thought of Joel Harcourt, the man she loved body and soul, the man who waited for her at the old parish church with its beautifully carved Norman arch and door, the man whose life would be forever linked with hers, Regina smiled. "Going to Brighton was the perfect plan."

WATCH FOR THESE REGENCY ROMANCES